Desires Of The Heart

A woman should have whatever her heart desires

Desires Of The Heart

A woman should have whatever her heart desires

Lisa Haynes

Dazzle Life Productions, LLC
Atlanta, GA 30350

ISBN 10: 0615286518
ISBN 13: 978-0-615-28651-8

First Dazzle Life Productions, LLC Edition, 2009

This book is dedicated to my beautiful and sweet mother, Bertha Haynes, Thank you for all the years filled with your love, sacrifices and guidance. You are an incredible woman and truly an angel. I love you.

And to my awesome and handsome son, Todd Jefferson, Jr. You are the greatest blessing God has ever given me. Thank you for being the best son a mother could ever ask for and for always trying to be the best that you can be. I love you with all my heart.

And to my wonderful husband, Andre Congo, Thank you for your love, support and encouragement. You truly are a dream come true.

ACKNOWLEDGEMENTS

I must first thank God for all the love and blessings He continues to bestow upon me. I know that I am nothing without you, Lord and I truly thank you for making all things possible in my life. Thank you for the special gift you have given me to be able to reach out and connect with others through my work as a journalist and an author. I pray that my work will continue to uplift and inspire others.

I want to thank my family and friends for continuing to encourage and support me every step of the way.

♥ _Chapter 1_ ♥

One side of the courtroom was packed full of family members of the late victim looking for someone to pay for their loss. On the other side sat those in support of the defendant, who believed the young black man was being accused of a murder he didn't commit. The tension in the courtroom was thick enough to cut with a knife.

The judge peered over the top of her eyeglasses. "Is the defense ready with closing arguments?" she asked.

Tony Boston whispered in his partner's ear and then stood. All eyes were on him, and why wouldn't they be? After all, he was just about as fine a black man as you could find. A six foot two, caramel brown–skinned, well-dressed brother with broad shoulders, wavy hair, a sexy smile, and more charm than any one man needed, Tony Boston made women melt.

He buttoned one of the buttons on his gray Armani suit jacket as he walked toward the jury. "Thank you, your honor," he said as he nodded to the judge. "Ladies and gentlemen of the jury, out of respect for your time and intelligence, I'm going to be as brief as possible here. Not to undermine the fact that indeed a terrible crime took place, but to make it very clear that my client is not and could not possibly be the one responsible. My client is very much an innocent man. Not only is Kevin Robinson an innocent man, he's a good man. He's twenty-six years old and just married his lovely young wife eight months ago, and they're now expecting their first child. Kevin is a churchgoing young man who loves the Lord. He works hard every day driving a delivery truck and then goes to school in the evening so he can complete his bachelor's degree in information technology. Kevin loves his wife and his mom and dad, and he's truly looking forward to being a father. There's nothing in him that would make him capable of such a crime."

Tony walked a little closer to the jury so he could look each member straight in the eye.

"Now that I've told you about the goodness of this young man, let me tell you why it is factually impossible that he could have committed this crime, and why there is an abundance of evidence that proves him not guilty. Let me say that again! There's an abundance of evidence that proves him not guilty!"

Tony concluded his closing arguments and took his seat. He looked over and tapped his client's hand as if to say, *Hang in there, buddy.* He then turned around to look at his client's young wife and gave her an encouraging smile.

Tony was much more than just a brilliant attorney. He seemed to have it all: good looks, his own law firm, a great family, wealth—and he was truly a sincere, caring person. He was used to fighting tough cases and winning, and he prayed that he'd win this one so that his young client could go home with his wife. Tony honestly believed his client was innocent; he would not have defended him if he'd thought for one second that he was guilty.

By 3:30 P.M. Friday afternoon the jury had been deliberating for more than five hours. Just as Tony started thinking deliberations might carry over to Monday, he heard someone yell, "The jury has reached a verdict!"

Tony looked at his partner, Mike, and then turned to Kevin.

"You ready, young man? Remember what I told you, just keep walking in faith and God will see you through. Come on, let's go in."

Kevin nodded his head to imply that he was ready to go back into the courtroom. He then looked up to heaven and whispered, "Please help me, God. Go in here with me, Jesus, and let me get the victory."

Tony opened the door to the courtroom and the three of them walked in.

"All rise!"

The judge entered the courtroom, took her seat, and turned to face the jury. "Ladies and gentlemen of the jury, have you reached a verdict?"

"We have, your honor!"

Kevin was silently whispering a prayer. All of a sudden, the words echoed throughout the chamber:

"We, the jury, find the defendant not guilty."

"Yes, Jesus!" Kevin yelled. "Thank you, Lord!"

Tears rolled down his cheeks as he reached over and hugged Tony. "Thank you so much, Mr. Boston. This wouldn't have happened without you, and I thank you for working so hard on this case."

"You're quite welcome, Kevin. You're a good young man and I thank God that the jury saw the truth. Now go on and get out of here and take care of that pregnant young wife of yours."

Kevin smiled. "Okay, Mr. Boston, you're the best!"

Tony shook his client's hand and then turned to Mike. "You ready to go?"

"Yeah, I'm ready, Tony. But I must admit, I was a little worried there for a minute. Weren't you?"

"Worried? Man, I'm Tony Boston. I rule the courtroom, what are you talking about, worried? I wasn't worried, but if I was a drinking man, I would sure be heading for a drink right about now." Both men laughed as they walked out of the courtroom.

"Oh, look here, Mike, don't forget Trey's Celebration party is tonight. Wow, I can't believe my son passed the bar. It's a dream come true, not just for him but for me too," Tony said.

"I'm very happy for you and your family. That's a big accomplishment. You know I'll be there," Mike said, as they headed down the hallway to the elevator.

♥ Chapter 2 ♥

Tony's oldest son, Trey, stood at the entrance of Emanuel's restaurant, an upscale black-owned steakhouse with a nightclub on the third floor. The décor was stunning with plush seats, several VIP sections, a built-in aquarium, marble floors, and spa-like restrooms. Everything about it was classy. The Boston family frequented the place for special occasions like birthdays, anniversaries, and other celebrations, and Trey's passing the bar and joining his father's law firm was definitely considered a special occasion.

Trey was twenty-nine years old and the spitting image of his father. He was handsome, sexy, charming, and had a gorgeous smile. When the two of them stood together, you could hardly tell them apart. Tony was more than two decades older than his son, but he could pass for Trey's older brother.

Trey's mother, Sheila, was a knockout, or as Trey's friends would always say, "She's bad!" She could pass for Trey's older sister if one didn't know any better.

Trey looked around the restaurant, catching a glimpse of the basketball game playing on one of the dozen plasma television sets. He stood there looking like a million bucks, dressed to impress in all black, with an attractive woman on his arm.

"Good evening Mr. Boston," the host said, "may I escort you to your table now?"

"Uh, yes, that's fine," Trey answered.

"Okay, Mr. Boston, right this way. Your party is in the VIP Grande section tonight."

Trey and his date walked into the plush section on the second floor, which boasted an impressive, wide-open view of the downstairs restaurant and the upstairs club.

"Whassup, Trey!" someone yelled from across the room. Trey looked over and saw his two best friends, Sean and Joe, sitting at the table with their dates.

"Hey man, whassup!" Trey said, smiling as he walked over to join them. "I can't believe you two are the first ones here. You finally made it somewhere on time," Trey said as everybody laughed. Trey introduced his date to his friends, and the two of them sat down.

The waitress had already started bringing hor d'oeuvres to the table when Trey's parents, Tony and Sheila, stepped in looking like a pair of movie stars. They were absolutely gorgeous. Sheila was light brown skin with nice curves, shoulder-length, reddish-brown hair and a beautiful smile. She was dressed in a spaghetti-strapped, knee-length black dress—stunning, and as classy as always. Tony, dressed in a black suit, looked like he'd just stepped off the cover of a magazine.

Their younger son, Todd walked in behind them. He was seventeen years old, and handsome just like his father. In fact, he looked just like a younger version of Trey. On a mission to impress his date for the evening, Todd made sure he was dressed to kill that night.

Kim, the family's twenty-seven-year-old housekeeper, also showed up. She'd been working for the family for the last ten years, ever since she used to watch Todd after school. The family loved her and decided to keep her on as their house-keeper when Todd got older. She was a nice, hard-working young lady. Even though she tried to hide it as much as she could, she had a serious crush on Trey and wanted a relationship with him. Trey had told her many times in the past that a relationship between them wouldn't work because he looked at her like a little sister—but the two of them had a little history together, which made being friends, difficult for Kim.

Everyone arrived and placed their orders and dinner was served. Not only did Emanuel's have incredible steaks, they had delicious seafood as well. Trey, Todd, and Tony each had the steak and lobster dinner. Sheila often marveled at how much her sons were just like their father, and looked just like him too.

Once all the food was on the table, Tony asked everyone to hold hands and bow their head as he said the blessing:

"Father God, in the name of Jesus we come to you in prayer, thanking you, Father God, for this blessed day, thanking you for this wonderful family, our friends and co-workers. Lord, this is quite a day for us—not only was a young man's life spared today in that courtroom, Father, but you have given us an incredible blessing in our family, allowing our Trey to pass the bar exam and become a lawyer; allowing us to be able to walk in your will and to continue to work to be a blessing to others. Father God, in the name of Jesus we thank you for this food and for all the blessings that you have bestowed upon us. We ask that you will continue to order our steps and guide our paths. We ask all these things in Jesus' name. Amen."

As the evening progressed, they enjoyed lots of laughs, excitement, and wonderful conversation. There were at least forty people at the celebration, mostly family members, close friends, and employees from Boston & Associates law firm. The firm was started by Tony more than fifteen years ago and was now considered one of the best in the state of Maryland.

As the guests finished their dinner, Tony tapped his spoon against his glass. "Okay, listen up, time for a toast."

Champagne was poured, and they all raised their glass as Tony began to speak. "Trey, son, I've always been so very proud of you. I'm proud of both you and Todd, of course. But what makes tonight so special is that you, my oldest son, have accomplished something truly impressive—you passed the bar exam. And now you have officially joined the family's business, Boston & Associates. Congratulations, son, and welcome aboard. Oh, and as a bonus, you'll begin working on your first case first thing Monday morning." Everyone laughed and shouted, "Here, here, congratulations!"

Trey's friend Sean, always the comedian in the bunch, waited for the crowd to take a sip of champagne and then added his two cents. "Look here, I would also like to pose a toast. To my boy Trey, man, our friendship goes back to the seventh grade, ever since the first time you walked into our homeroom class and got cracked on because everybody thought you had a Geri curl." Everyone in the room laughed hysterically.

"I would just like to say you are and always have been someone who wanted to accomplish great things in life and always wanted to be the best that you could be, and you really helped keep me and Joe on the right track. So tonight I say congratulations on your huge success, and I'll be there to congratulate you each and every time you win a case in the courtroom. Oh, and I still owe you a butt kicking for stealing my girlfriend in the tenth grade. Don't think I forgot about that." Everyone laughed as they raised their champagne to toast.

As the night continued, Trey's date started to feel uncomfortable as she noticed Kim staring at her. It was obvious that Kim was staring because she wished she could be the one who was hugged up with Trey. Trey's date was not someone he was seeing on a regular basis, just a former law school classmate he'd invited because he needed a date and she happened to be a nice young-lady.

At about 10:30 P.M. Trey decided to move the party to the club upstairs, where they were once again given VIP seats. Many guests hit the dance floor, and they all seemed to be having a good time.

Plenty of men asked Kim if she wanted to dance, but she turned them all down. She was hoping Trey would ask her to hit the floor with him. After all, Kim was very attractive, with nice curves. She was about five feet eight, brown skin with long hair and a sweet personality. What else could Trey want?

Trey and his date stayed on the dance floor for three songs straight before coming back to the table. At that point a beautiful young lady who'd been eying Trey from across the room came over and stood next to him.

"Hello," the stranger said as she flashed a flirtatious smile at the man of the hour.

"Hello," Trey said.

"I don't mean to interrupt, but I couldn't help but overhear that congratulations are in order for a new attorney here at this table."

"Yeah, that's right," Trey said, smiling.

"Well, my name is Kendra and I'm actually here celebrating something similar. I just got accepted into law school, so I wanted to come over and say congratulations and that I admire you for completing the journey that I'm about to embark on. So enjoy your celebration and I wish you much success," she said, smiling.

"Oh, okay, thank you, thank you very much, and I wish you much success as well, Kendra. It was nice of you to come over." Trey smiled, trying to pretend he wasn't blown away by how beautiful she was. As Kendra walked away, Trey, Sean, and Joe all took a glance, then gave each other that look that silently said she was gorgeous.

As the night was coming to an end, Kendra ran into Trey as he was walking out of the men's room.

"Hello again," Kendra said, smiling.

"Hey," Trey replied.

"Uh, I don't know if that's your girlfriend with you, but I was wondering if you would like to dance with me."

"No, she's not my girl, but she is my date for the evening and I think it might be a little disrespectful for me to dance with another woman."

"Yeah, you're right. By the way, you never told me your name." Kendra moved a little closer to him.

"Oh, excuse my rudeness, I'm Trey, and, uh, you said you were celebrating tonight. Where's the rest of your party?"

"It's just me and a few of my girlfriends, and right now they're spread out on the floor dancing."

This second meeting gave Trey a chance to really see how attractive Kendra was, and he was making no bones about checking her out. She was a light-skinned woman, about five seven with a medium frame and nice curves, and she had long black hair, a killer smile, and a sex appeal that he could see right away.

"Well, look Kendra, since I can't dance with you tonight, how about I give you a rain check. Do you have a number where I can reach you, and maybe I'll take you someplace where we can dance. Would you like that?"

"Yes, I would. That sounds very nice." Kendra wrote down her number and handed it to him.

"Do you have a number?" she asked.

"I sure do." He pulled out one of his new business cards from his father's law firm.

"My goodness, I see you're already official, Mr. Attorney," Kendra said as she read the card. "Well, thank you and I hope to hear from you soon, Trey." She walked away.

"I look forward to talking to you soon, Kendra," Trey said,

watching as she walked away.

Trey made his way back to the table. He smiled at his parents as they returned from the dance floor.

"Whew! Son, we're going to get out of here," Tony said.

"Yeah, baby, we just danced for three straight songs, and that's enough for these old feet," Sheila said as they all laughed. Tony and Sheila said goodbye to everyone. They asked Todd to give Kim a ride back to her apartment because she wasn't quite ready to leave with them.

As Trey sat down at the table, his eyes scanned the room, hoping to catch another glimpse of Kendra.

During the ride home, Tony hinted around that he wanted to get intimate with his wife.

"I told you about eating all those oysters. I think they're more than just your favorite appetizer," Sheila said, smiling at her husband,

"Oysters? It's not the oysters, baby, it's the way you were dancing tonight that turned me on." He rubbed her shoulder.

Tony parked in their garage and let his wife out of the car. He was always quite the gentlemen.

Tony started kissing Sheila as soon as they walked into the house.

"Oh my! What's gotten into you? You barely let me get in the door." Sheila pushed him away so she could walk into the kitchen.

"That's nothing, baby, just wait until I get you upstairs," he said as he tapped her on the bottom. "Baby you were looking real sexy out there on that dance floor. I couldn't believe that was wife moving around like one of those girls in the music videos."

"Oh please, Tony, I was not dancing like the girls in the videos. But it's nice to know I can still get my husband's attention when I want to." Sheila put her hand on her hip.

She turned out the kitchen light and made her way upstairs to the bedroom, with Tony following closely behind.

"You are something else, woman," he said as they made their way into their bedroom.

Tony began to take off his clothes as Sheila stood in front of the mirror taking off her jewelry.

He walked over and slipped his arms around her waist. She turned to face him as they looked deep into each other's eyes. Tony was always so romantic. He kissed his wife softly "I love you, Mrs. Boston," he said as he nibbled on her ear.

"I love you too, Mr. Boston."

♥ Chapter 3 ♥

Kim brushed butter on the final batch of biscuits after pulling them from the oven. She loved weekend mornings at the Boston house because they always started with a big family breakfast and that was her specialty. Todd was the first one downstairs and went out to the patio table. When he was younger he used to like to sleep late on Saturday mornings, but since the Boston family started their Big Breakfast Weekends tradition, he was usually the first one at the table. Todd was just as cute as he could be and loved to eat.

"Good morning, Kim," Todd said. He took his favorite seat next to his mother's chair.

"Good morning, Todd," Kim said as she placed the piping hot biscuits directly in front of him.

"That's right, put them right here." Todd rubbed his hands together like he couldn't wait to sink his teeth into them. "You know the smell of your first batch of biscuits is what wakes me up in the morning. They just be calling me, for real."

Todd was a big ole momma's boy at heart and the girls at school loved him. His mother always talked about how their home phone immediately rang every time he decided not to answer his cell phone. But just like their dad, both Todd and Trey seemed to be what you'd call a one-woman man, and that made their mom proud of her sons.

One by one members of the family came to the table. Sheila and Tony came down together, and Trey was the last one to sit down, probably because he was the last one to get home from his celebration the night before.

Trey actually lived in the in-law suite, which was attached to the main house. He'd previously owned a townhouse, but sold it and moved back to his parents' house while he finished law school, so he could save some money for a bigger house.

"Good morning, people," Trey said as he sat down across from Todd. During the summer they mostly ate their big breakfasts out back near the pool. They lived a nice life of luxury, but were modest about it. They enjoyed nice things, but spent money wisely and were quite humble and always gave thanks to God for everything.

Kim placed the bowl of eggs on the table, then sat down and joined the family. They treated her just like she was a Boston herself. Kim had her own apartment and was in school studying nursing. Sometimes she spent the night at the Bostons' house and even had her own room.

"Girl, you sure will make some lucky man a good husband, the way you can cook, um huh um," Trey said as he started in on his plate.

"Oh yeah, you know any nice available men, because I'm definitely looking." Kim said, looking at Trey with her eyebrows raised.

Tony noticed her look and laughed, then looked at Trey.

"Well Trey, do you know anybody you think would make a nice young man for Kim?"

"Actually I do. My boy Sean is crazy about her." Trey laughed.

"Sean, that nut? I wouldn't go out with Sean if he paid me," Kim said.

"What's wrong with Sean? He's cool. He's well-established, with a good career as a high school football coach making alright money, plus he has a good head on his shoulders and he really wants to get with you." Trey said as he stuffed his face.

"No thanks. Besides, I have somebody in mind already and I'm praying that God will bring us together," Kim said with a big smile on her face.

"Oh yeah, and who is this somebody?" Trey asked, looking at Kim with one eyebrow raised.

The other three at the table tried to hold back their giggles. They were well aware that Kim was talking about Trey. Kim had made it known on several occasions in the past that she wanted to be Trey's woman.

"Why are you worried about who it is Trey? Are you jealous?" Everybody laughed.

"No, I'm not jealous, just curious," Trey said.

"Obviously you're not curious enough," Kim mumbled under her breath.

Tony decided now would be a good time to break up the conversation before it went too far. "So how about those Ravens? They sure can play some football, huh," Tony said, interrupting.

Trey laughed and decided it was best to change the subject. "So Todd, are you looking forward to spending the next four years in the ATL?" Trey asked.

"Oh yeah," Todd said, still throwing down on his food. "I'm glad you and Dad talked me into going to Morehouse. I've been hearing nothing but good things about it and the ATL sounds like it's definitely the place to be. Not to mention all those Spelman girls I'm going to be just a hop, skip, and a jump away from." Todd laughed.

"You know that's how I met your mother. She was a Spellman girl," Tony said.

"Oh come on, Dad, not this story again," Todd said. Every

body at the table laughed.

"Leave your father alone, Todd," Sheila said. "My hubby loves telling stories about our college days. After all, they were fun and exciting. We were both pretty popular on campus, and right there in the heart of Atlanta is where your father and I fell in love." Sheila leaned over and kissed Tony.

Trey jumped in. "Todd, I'm telling you, you can't go wrong with Morehouse, man, I had a good time when I was there. Unfortunately I didn't meet the future Mrs. Trey Boston there, although there were a lot of prospects," Trey said as he sucked his teeth.

"I can't wait to get there," Todd said.

Tony put his hand on Todd's shoulder and got that *Dad is about to give some advice* look on his face. "Look here, boy, like I told you plenty of times before, you're not going to Morehouse for the Spelman girls, you're going to Morehouse to get a wonderful education from an excellent college. Now it just so happens that I met my wife at Spelman, but there's no guarantee that will happen for you, and that is not to be your focus. Your focus is your education. You understand?"

"Yes sir," Todd said.

"How come you two came to Maryland to live and didn't stay in Atlanta?" Kim asked, looking at Tony and Sheila.

"Well," Sheila started, "I'm originally from New York and Tony is of course from Maryland, so we wanted to come back up North, and since Maryland is such a beautiful place, we settled here. I mean, we both love Atlanta, which is why we often visit, and I'm really looking forward to driving Todd down to Morehouse like we did Trey."

"Yeah, Atlanta is nice. I think Todd will really like it," Kim said.

"I can't believe my baby is all grown up and going to college," Sheila said as she pinched his cheek.

"I know Ma, I can't wait."

"Kim, breakfast was delicious as usual, but I've got to get

going so I'll catch y'all later." Trey said as he stood up and excused himself from the table.

"I'd better get going too," Sheila said, getting up from the table. "I need to get to the spa and check on the new ladies I hired. It's their first day and I want to make sure they get off to a good start." She was the owner of a day spa called Paradise. "What are you guys doing today?" Sheila asked.

"I'm going to get my brakes fixed, then to the movies later," Todd said.

"I'm going to head to the office and get a jump on this case I just started," Tony replied..

"I'm going to clean up around here, then go to my apartment and get some homework done," Kim said.

"Well, sounds like everybody's got something going on, so be careful, and baby, I'll see you tonight." Sheila leaned over and kissed Tony.

Kim watched Trey as he walked into the house. *How can I get this man to pay more attention to me,* she thought, as she started clearing the table.

♥ Chapter 4 ♥

*I*t was Monday morning and Trey was dressed and ready for his first day of work as an attorney at Boston & Associates. He went over to the main house to talk to his dad before heading to work. Trey walked into his old bedroom and stood in front of the mirror as he straightened his necktie. He couldn't help but think about how fast the weekend had gone by, probably because he'd really been anticipating his first day. "Hey Ma, come here," he yelled. Luckily everybody in the house was already awake, because his old bedroom was quite a ways from his parents' room and yet Sheila still heard him.

"What's the matter?" She walked toward his room.

"Come here, look," he said, motioning his mother to come over to the full-length mirror.

"Look at what, Trey?"

"Look at how fine I am. Now, you can't tell me I don't look like an attorney."

Sheila laughed. "Boy, you are a mess. Yes, you do look fine, son, and I must say you sure do look like an attorney," Sheila said as she straightened his tie. "Tony," she yelled as she walked back to her room, "That son of yours is crazy and he gets it from his father."

"Trey, come on, you might as well ride with me to the office so I can take you around and help you get settled in for your first day," Tony said.

"Alright Dad, but let me drive. That's the least I can do since you hired me and everything," Trey said.

"Okay son, that's cool, that's cool."

When Trey pulled onto the parking lot of the law firm, he saw a parking spot with his name on it, Trey V. Boston.

"Surprise," Tony said.

"Aw man, that's alright, Dad. I feel real official now," Trey said, grinning from ear to ear.

"Alright son, let's go."

They walked in the door of the downtown office. The office, located in the heart of downtown Baltimore, was absolutely beautiful. Trey was given a corner office, opposite Tony's office, and they both had spectacular views overlooking the Inner Harbor.

Tony was introduced to his secretary, Teresa. A young, pretty, dark-skinned girl with braids, Teresa was very professional and efficient. She was selected as Trey's secretary by Tony's secretary, Linda, who was the absolute best. Linda knew Teresa would make sure Trey was well taken care of and would do an excellent job.

Trey walked into his office, looked around, and was then invited to a meeting in the boardroom. Everyone was asked to do what they could to help him during his first few weeks. Trey then found out that he'd be working on a big case with his father.

It was late afternoon and Trey was in his office reading over some case files when his secretary buzzed his phone. "Mr. Boston, I have a Miss Kendra on the line for you," she said.

Trey thought for a moment, then told his secretary to put the call through.

"Hello," he said.

"Hi Trey, this is Kendra, the woman you met the other night at Emanuel's."

"Hello, Kendra."

"I hope this isn't a bad time, but I just wanted to call and wish you well on your first day as a new lawyer."

"Oh, well, thank you, thank you very much. How'd you know it was my first day?" Trey asked.

"I overheard your dad telling one of his friends at the party."

"Oh, okay."

"So how's your first day going?" She asked.

"It's pretty good. I already have my own parking spot, a corner office overlooking the Inner Harbor, and an efficient secretary, so I'm all set."

"Wow, sounds nice. I guess you are set. So have you had lunch?" Kendra asked.

"We had a meeting and lunch was ordered, so I already ate."

"Too bad, I was hoping I could treat you to lunch for your first day," She replied.

"Well, I'll still need to eat dinner later on. How about dinner?" He asked.

"That would be nice."

"Okay, I can pick you up, do you work downtown?"

"Yes, I do. I work at a bank in the heart of downtown, at One Hundred West Charles Street."

"That's not too far at all. What time do you get off?" Trey asked.

"I get off at five."

"Cool, I'll be leaving here at about four thirty, so I'll swing by and get you."

"Okay, what kind of car are you driving so I'll know what to look for?"

"I'm driving a black BMW, with Boston 3 on the tag."

"Okay, I'll see you then," Kendra said.

Trey hung up the phone and then remembered that he drove

his father to work. He called his father's office. "Hey Dad, can you see if Mom can pick you up from the office? Something just came up that I need to do after work," Trey said, hoping his father wouldn't mind.

"Yeah, that shouldn't be a problem," Tony said.

"Alright, Dad, thanks."

"No problem, Son. So tell me how's your first day been so far?"

"Very nice, thanks for everything. And hopefully my day is about to get even better."

"Oh, that's why you can't take me home? I meant to tell you that the ladies have a thing for attorneys, but I guess you're already starting to find out," Tony said. "Goodbye, Son."

Both men laughed and hung up the phone.

♥ <u>Chapter 5</u> ♥

*T*rey pulled up in front of the office building. He saw Kendra standing outside in a lavender dress and a pair of high heels. "Whew, she's fine," he said out loud, shaking his head. He pulled the car next to the curb and got out to open the door for her. "Hello, Miss," he said, noticing once again how pretty she was.

"Hello Trey, it's good to see you again." Kendra flashed her pretty smile.

"It's good to see you too." He opened the passenger side door to let Kendra in. *Um huh um,* he thought when he got a glimpse of her legs.

Trey then got back in the car and pulled off. "So how long have you been with the bank?" he asked.

"For about two years. It's just something to pay the bills for now until I get through law school and become a big-time attorney like you," She replied.

"So what kind of attorney do you want to be?" he asked.

"I want to be a criminal defense attorney like you and your dad."

"So you know a little something about us, I see."

"As much as your father has been in the news, anybody would know would about him. He has an incredible reputation of being a winner, but also of being a very upstanding, respectable man," she said.

"Yeah, that's my Dad, and that's exactly the kind of attorney I aspire to be," Trey said, smiling proudly.

"So tell me Kendra, do you like seafood?"

"I sure do. I like all kinds of food. It's a wonder I'm not as big as a house, the way I like to eat."

"So if you like to eat so much, how do you keep that beautiful body of yours?" Trey asked, taking advantage of the opportunity to give her a good look over.

"Well, I think I've figured out a little something that works for me. I try to eat oatmeal every morning since it has lots of fiber, and I do a workout tape at least three times a week, plus I get low-fat this and that whenever I can, and I don't eat butter unless it's fat-free margarine, no soda, and I drink lots of water. So it does require me to work out and to watch what I eat, even though I splurge a lot. But thank you for the compliment. You have a nice body yourself, Mr. Boston. Do you work out?"

"I have a membership at a gym. I probably go twice a week. Most of my exercise comes from playing basketball. Me and my boys Sean and Joe, the two who were at the party the other night, play ball like twice a week and we play for about three hours at a time. We're on a team that plays in Ellicott City each week."

"So can you play?" She looked over at him smiling.

"I can do a little somethin'-somethin' on the court. Now my boy Sean, you can't tell him he's not Michael Jordan. He thinks he's the best thing out there," He said, laughing.

Trey pulled into the valet parking lot of a nice seafood restaurant, which was located not too far from downtown. Once they were out of the car, he escorted his date inside. It didn't take long for them to be seated, and they both started with an order of   steamed shrimp. Trey told her all about his family and how proud he was of his younger brother, Todd, who was about to go to Atlanta to attend Morehouse College, the same college he and his father attended.

Kendra didn't talk much about her family. She told Trey she was an only child and that her mother was killed in a car accident several years ago. She also told him her father lived in Illinois and that she didn't see him very often. Kendra told him that she was born in Maryland and had recently graduated from college with a bachelor's degree.

"So why do you want to be a lawyer?" Trey asked.

"I think far too many innocent people get sent to jail for crimes they didn't commit, and I want to do what I can to keep that from happening," Kendra replied.

"Wow, that's really admirable of you," Trey said.

As the evening continued they talked and laughed a lot and enjoyed each other's company. They were having such a great time that they didn't realize how late it was.

"Well, it's almost ten o'clock, Kendra. I should get you home, plus I have a big day tomorrow," Trey said.

"Wow, I had no idea it was so late. I guess time flies when you're having fun," Kendra said smiling at Trey.

"Guess so."

Trey motioned to the waiter to bring the check. He settled the bill and they headed out front and waited for the attendant to get the car. Once they were back in the car, Trey put in a Maxwell CD and opened the sunroof.

"So did you park your car downtown or did you take the subway to work?" He asked.

"I drove, so you can just take me back to the garage at my building and I'll drive home."

"Where do you live? I can follow you home to make sure you get in safely," he said.

"Oh that's so sweet of you, but I'll be fine. I live in Towson and it's a pretty safe area, so I'll be okay," she replied.

Trey pulled into the parking garage of Kendra's job. She pointed out a gold-tone Honda Accord as her car. Trey got out and opened her door.

"Thank you so much for a nice evening, Trey," she said as she stepped out.

"And thank you for your company and for the good conversation," Trey said.

Kendra could sense that Trey wanted a kiss. Maybe it was his body language and the fact that he was standing so close to her, or perhaps it was the fact that his eyes appeared to be glued to her lips. She knew her assumptions were right when Trey leaned in and quickly kissed her on the cheek. Kendra pulled back. "Wow, thanks."

"Okay Kendra, you be careful driving home."

"Good night, Trey," Kendra said as she smiled and started her car. She waved goodbye and pulled off. *Boy, this is not going to be easy. He seems like a really nice guy. I don't know if I can go through with this,* she thought.

♥ _Chapter 6_ ♥

"Right here, Trey, right here," Sean hollered as the boys played ball on the court. Trey passed the ball to Sean and he hit a three pointer.

"What, what!," Sean said, obviously grand standing. He was a really good ballplayer and very dramatic on the court. Trey and Sean usually played on the same team, while their boy Joe played against them. All three were good, but Sean often scored the most points when they played.

The three of them sat down to take a break. "Hey, you'll never guess who I went out with last night," Trey said with a smile.

"Who?" Joe asked.

"Remember that pretty young-lady from Emanuel's the other night?"

"Which one? There were a whole lot of pretty women at Emanuel's the other night. In fact, there was nothing but pretty women there the other night," Sean said as he leaned over to tie his tennis shoe.

"I'm talking about the one who came over to the table to say congratulations to me," Trey bounced the ball in between his legs.

"What, you went out with her? How did you hook up with her?" Joe asked.

"I didn't tell you all, but when I went to the bathroom later that night, I bumped into her again and we exchanged numbers, and then she called me yesterday to see how my first day of work was going and we hooked up." Trey gave them a look that said, *Yeah, I'm the man.*

"Man, she's bad!" Joe said.

"Yeah man, I was planning on going back to the club to see if I could find her myself," Sean said, laughing.

"Well, too late playa, I'm on it now, so back off." Trey smirked.

"So what's up with her?" Joe asked.

"From what she tells me, she's single, no kids, about to start law school, works downtown at a bank, and lives in an apartment in Towson. She seems real cool. Oh, did I mention, she's just as fine as she can be and intelligent too," Trey added.

"So how was it?" Sean said, with a big, dumb smile.

"Real nice, she's seems pretty cool. I definitely want to see her again. I plan to take things really slow. I'm at the point where I'm looking to settle down soon, and I ain't playing no games with these women out here. I'm looking for a wife. I'm looking for the woman who will become Mrs. Trey Boston, so I can start a family." Trey spun the ball on his index finger.

"Whoa, whoa, whoa, slow down playa. A wife? Man, what are you talking about? The three of us said we wouldn't even think about making that kind of move until we were at least thirty-five. You still got at least another five or six years to go." Sean snatched the ball from Trey.

"Look, I know a good thing when I see it, and if this woman is all she seems to be, she could be Mrs. Trey Boston. You two can do whatever." Trey snatched the ball back.

"Well, I know I'm not looking to get married anytime soon.

Besides, there are too many honeys out there," Sean said.

"I don't know, Sean. I'm feeling like Trey a little bit. I mean, if the right woman comes along and I really feel like she's sent from God, then I would consider going all the way too," Joe said.

"Man, y'all some suckers. All I know is I still got at least five more years of the bachelor life in me, and I'm gonna enjoy it." Sean said as he strolled back on to the court.

♥ <u>Chapter 7</u> ♥

Trey was sitting in the boardroom of Boston & Associates when he felt his cell phone vibrating. He reached down to check the number and saw that it was Kendra. He couldn't answer it because he was in the middle of a meeting with a client, but he was glad that she called because he'd been thinking about her since their dinner two nights ago.

When the meeting was over, Trey pulled out his phone as he walked back to his office, and returned her call. It rang twice before she answered.

"Hello."

"Hello Miss, this is Trey."

"Hi Trey, how are you?"

"I'm good, how are you?"

"I'm fine," she said.

"Yes, you are," he said. He heard her giggle. "So did I catch you at a bad time?"

"No, not at all, I was actually just wrapping up things here at work and about to head home," she replied.

"I'm about to leave work myself. Are you hungry?"

"I'm always hungry, believe it not." Kendra laughed.

"Well, that's a good thing because I'm always hungry too. I was thinking about grabbing a bite to eat right now. Would you like to join me?" Trey asked.

"Sure I would."

"Alright, I'll pick you up at about five. Does that work?" Trey asked.

"Sure does. I'll see you then."

Trey pulled up in front of Kendra's office and saw her standing outside talking to a co-worker. *Umm-huh-um, she looks good,* he thought, as he noticed her nicely fitting red dress, high-heeled shoes, and red lipstick. He put the car in park, got out, and walked around to the passenger side. As Kendra walked over with a big smile on her face, Trey opened his arms, motioning that he wanted a hug, and she just seemed to naturally fall into them. It was obvious they were happy to see each other.

"You look very nice today, Miss," Trey said as he stepped back and checked her out.

"Thank you,and you're looking rather handsome yourself, sir," Kendra said batting her eyelashes.

"So what do you have a taste for?" Trey asked as he let her into the car.

"I could go for Mexican tonight," she said.

"Mexican, huh, alright, I can go for that," Trey said.

Kendra directed him to a nice Mexican restaurant located close to her apartment. Once there, they asked the waiter to seat them at an outdoor table.

Once again the conversation was great. They started to get into some more serious questions like future plans, whether each had a desire to get married and have kid as well as likes and dislikes. All the questions that seem to say, *I'm interested, let me hear more about you,* and so far they both liked the answers. They each expressed a desire to marry and have kids in the future. Kendra said she didn't want any more than

three kids, Trey said no more than two. As the night continued, Trey felt himself staring at Kendra quite a bit. He was not
only intrigued by her beauty, he also really enjoyed being in
her company and thought she seemed very down to earth and
interesting.

The two of them enjoyed their meal and conversation so
much they didn't want to call it a night, even though it was
getting late. After about three hours at the restaurant, Kendra
knew she had to go so she could get up in the morning.

"Once again you've talked my ear off, but I think we'd better
call it a night," she said with a smile.

"I don't think so, Miss Lady. You'd better change that to you
talking *my* ear off, as most women do." Trey laughed. "No, seriously, I had a nice time with you once again, Kendra. You'd
better watch out, I could really get used to this," He said, smiling.

"Well, I hope you will. I think that would be a good thing."
She smiled back.

Trey insisted on not taking Kendra all the way back downtown when they were so close to her apartment. He told her
he would take her home and then pick her up in the morning.
He said he would give her a ride to work. That way she could
leave her car at the office and let him take her home tonight.
After going back and forth a couple of times, Kendra finally
agreed.

When they arrived at her apartment, Trey walked her to the
door and stood behind her while she searched her purse for
her keys.

"You should always have your keys in your hand and ready
when you get to your door," Trey said, shaking his head in
disbelief at how long she was scrambling for her keys.

She turned around to face him. "Well, usually I have my keys
out because I drive myself home, and I always have my door
key ready as I approach my apartment. I live alone—even
though Towson is a nice area and is relatively safe, I'm not

naïve when it comes to protecting myself. But thanks for your concern." She tilted her head slightly as if to say, *I got this!*

Trey just smiled, acknowledging that Miss Kendra was a woman who seemed to speak her mind, and what a strong mind it was. He found that very attractive.

She opened the door and stepped inside.

"Would you like to come in and search the apartment to make sure I'm safe?" She said with a sarcastic tone. "No, I'm kidding. I'm fine, Mr. Boston, and thanks again for a lovely evening. What time are you picking me up in the morning?"

"Well, since I need to be at the office no later than eight, how about I pick you up at 7:15, is that cool?"

"Cool with me."

Trey leaned in and kissed Kendra on the lips. She responded by kissing him back. "I think I'd better let you go inside before I get carried away," Trey said as he stepped back slightly.

"Alright, hot lips, I'll see you in the morning." She flashed her pretty smile as she closed the door.

"Good night," he replied.

As Trey was driving home his cell phone rang. He looked down and saw it was Kendra calling, and he blushed.

He answered. "Hello."

"Hi, it's Kendra. Look, I know this is an absolute no-no in the rules of dating, but I just wanted to call and say I had a really nice time with you tonight and that I look forward to going out with you again."

"Who said we were dating?" Trey said and could almost hear her embarrassment over the phone. "I'm just kidding Kendra," he said, laughing. "I had a nice time with you as well, alright, now get some sleep so you can be ready when I come get you in the morning."

"Okay, Trey goodnight."

"Goodnight," he said, smiling as he hung up the phone. *She seems really cool, I like a woman who doesn't seem to have any drama,* he thought.

♥ <u>Chapter 8</u> ♥

$\mathcal{K}$endra sat on her bed staring at her cell phone. She started laughing when she thought about what he'd just said to her. She thought he was really a funny guy, not to mention handsome, smart, down-to-earth, a go-getter, and a member of a very successful family.

Kendra's smile soon faded as she picked up a photo from her end table. It was a picture of her as a young girl with her mother and father. She ran her finger across her mother's face and whispered, "Oh mom, I miss you so much. Not a day goes by that I don't think about you and wish I could talk to you about life." A few tears came as she ran her finger across her dad's face in the photo.

"Daddy, I love you. I just hope I can do what you're asking me to do. You'll be proud to know that I've made the first step in avenging the wrong that Tony Boston did to you.

♥ ♥ ♥ ♥ ♥ ♥ ♥ ♥ ♥ ♥ ♥ ♥ ♥ ♥ ♥ ♥ ♥ ♥

Kendra's cell phone rang at 7:10 Friday morning.

"Hello," she said.

"Good morning, Kendra, this is Trey."

"Good morning, Trey."

"I'll be pulling up to your apartment in about five minutes, are you ready?" he asked.

"Yes, I'm ready."

"Okay, I'll see you in a few."

When Trey pulled up to Kendra's apartment she was standing outside.

"That's my girl, always ready, I like that," he said out loud, while still in the car.

Kendra opened the door and got in before Trey could get out.

"I like the fact that you're always ready and don't leave a brother waiting," he said smiling. He considered giving her a kiss but thought that might be a bit much—after all, they'd only been on two dates.

"So how are you doing this morning?" he asked, looking over at her.

"I'm fine, and you?"

"Oh, I'm good."

Trey couldn't help but notice that she didn't seem quite the same. For some reason she just wasn't the happy-spirited young lady he'd seen over the last couple of days. *Maybe she's not a morning person,* he thought.

The ride downtown was quiet, and Trey noticed that Kendra mostly stared out of the passenger-side window.

"So do you have a big day ahead?" Trey asked trying to break the silence.

"Uh, no, today it should be pretty quiet actually. In fact, I'm leaving work early because I have an appointment."

It was obvious that Kendra had something on her mind, but Trey didn't push the issue.

Once they arrived at her office building, he said goodbye and told her to have a good day. He also asked her to call him later if she had a chance.

Trey watched her walk inside and was surprised that she didn't turn around to wave goodbye. *Maybe she's upset about my little joke last night on the phone. Maybe she's just not feeling me. I hope that's not it,* he thought as he pulled off.

♥ <u>Chapter 9</u> ♥

 Kendra left work early and headed to the prison to see her father. He'd been locked up for the past twelve years and she faithfully visited him every week. She thought this visit might be a little different from all the rest because for the first time in her life, she wanted to stand up to her father and tell him what was on her mind.

Kendra waited nervously for him to come into the visiting area. As she sat there, she saw his cellmate, Wayne, come out to meet with his wife. Wayne was so happy to see his wife that he didn't notice Kendra. A few minutes later, Rob came out and hugged Kendra, obviously happy to see her. As soon as Rob sat down, he could tell something was on his daughter's mind.

"What's wrong baby?" Rob asked.

"Daddy, I want to talk to you about something," she said, hesitating before continuing. "You know I love you, and I told you that I would always be there for you. I also promised you that I would take care of something for you, but I've changed my mind about it. See Daddy, I've been going to church lately and praying a lot and really working on my relationship with God, and it has made me think twice about what you've asked me to do. I just don't think it's right that you want me to trick the Boston family into thinking that I'm falling in love with Trey, and then bring their family down. I just don't think that's right. I mean, I feel bad that you're in here, but I know that God expects me to be honest in all things—and besides, I like Trey. He seems really nice."

Rob just sat there for a few minutes and didn't say a word. He looked at Kendra with disgust.

"What do you mean you like Trey and he seems nice? The hell with Trey and everybody else in that damn Boston family. Do I need to remind you that we had a great family until that double-crossing Tony Boston turned on me in the middle of my rape trial? Here he was supposed to be my lawyer and a friend of mine. He was the best lawyer in town, had never lost a case, and hasn't lost another one since mine. But he decides in the middle of my trial that he wants to believe the victim, that stupid girl who accused me of raping her. I never touched that silly girl. I was happily married to your mother and loved my daughter. I wouldn't have done anything to jeopardize that. But because this stupid girl didn't get an A in my class, she cries rape and Tony Boston believes her. I don't have anything but harsh feelings towards that man. I want his family to fall apart just like my family did.

"Do I need to remind you, Kendra, that I have been in prison for twelve years? Do I need to remind you that your mother died because she was so distraught when I was sentenced to jail and got behind the wheel of the car trying to make it home but crashed and died instead? How do you think I have felt all these years, being here in jail, my wife dead and my daughter's out there all alone? It kills me, Kendra, and somebody is gonna pay for this.

"Now you need to pull yourself together and stick to the plan. I want you to make Trey fall in love with you, then get close to the rest of the Boston family and let them trust you. Make sure all your legal documents have been changed to your aunt's last name, Jackson, and do not use our real last name, Stewart. I want you to set Tony Boston up and make it look like he tried to rape you and make sure that Trey is so in love with you that he will side with you and not his father. And don't forget to do things to make his wife think that he's having an affair. Huh, truth be told, Sheila wanted me anyway. She was dating me in college first, before Tony came along. So yeah, I've got a lot to pay that bastard back for. Now pull yourself together, young lady, because it's time to do what we've been talking about doing for years. And just think, I have less than twenty months left in this place and then we can have the type of life that I always wanted for our family; only it will be just me and you and not your mom. And of course I can never go back to being a college professor, but we'll have a happy life anyway. Come on, Kendra, you can do this." Rob rubbed her shoulder.

Kendra and Rob were so engrossed in their conversation that they didn't realize that Wayne was listening. Not only was Wayne Rob's cellmate, he was basically the only friend Rob had in that place. Rob had talked to Wayne about the whole Tony Boston situation and Wayne told Rob that he thought he was way too obsessed with wanting to get revenge on Tony. Rob often talked to Wayne about how he would not rest until that man paid for what he'd done to him.

Kendra felt tears coming to her eyes but didn't want to cry in front of her father. She gathered her things and told him that she would go along with the plan. A few minutes later they hugged and said goodbye.

Once inside her car she broke down and cried. It was all just too much for her to deal with. There was so much pain inside of her from her family's past. She was just fifteen when her father was sent to jail and her mother was killed.

Before all that, the Stewarts had a wonderful life. Her father treated her like a princess, but she had sometimes heard her mother and father arguing about him having an affair. She was close to her father, and he was a well-liked professor at the university he worked at in Baltimore. Kendra's mom was a high school principal and her staff and students were devastated by the news of her tragic death. Twelve years later, Kendra was still carrying around a lot of hurt and pain from the loss of her mother and her father being behind bars. She spent years in counseling and had been doing very well for the last three years. She moved out of her aunt's house into her own apartment, graduated from college, and had been accepted into law school. Kendra wanted so desperately to live a normal life, but her father made her feel guilty for it.

Kendra wiped her eyes as she sat in the car, and her thoughts started drifting to Trey. She thought about not seeing him again; then she could just tell her father that Trey wasn't really interested in her because he was seeing some other girl. Kendra knew that Trey was someone whom she could really fall for, and she didn't want to take that chance. She knew in her heart that the best thing to do was to just leave Trey Boston alone.

♥ *Chapter 10* ♥

*T*rey couldn't help but think about Kendra throughout the day, while he was at work. As he wrapped up things at the office, he wondered why he hadn't heard from her all day. He also wondered if something was bothering her because she was so quiet in the car during the drive to work, and did not seem like herself at all. He wanted to call her but didn't want to seem pushy or like he was falling for her too fast. He decided to wait until he heard from her. Besides, he'd already made plans to hang out and go to the game after work with his boys.

Just as Trey was about to shut down his computer for the day, Todd walked into his office.

"Whassup, man," Trey said, happy to see his younger brother.

"Hey, whassup Trey? Man, look at this office. This is nice. You got a corner office just like Dad, what's up with that? I thought you had to work your way up to that." Todd said as he looked around Trey's office in amazement.

"What can I say, man, Dad knows what he's doing. He knows I'm the next Tony Boston, the one who's gonna tear it up in the courtroom just like his father does." Trey smiled.

A few minutes later Sean and Joe walked in.

"Whassup?" they shouted as everybody shook hands.

"So how did you all get in here and the guard didn't buzz me not once?
A brother gets a corner office and suddenly gets no respect, what's up with that?" Trey said. The guys all laughed.

"Alright, y'all ready to go to this game or what?" Sean said, walking over to Todd. "Todd, look here man, stick with me, I'm gonna show you how to pull all the honeys." He put his arm around Todd.

"Show me?" Todd said. "Man, I'm seventeen years old. I don't need no help pulling women. In fact, I don't need to pull them anyway, they always come to me trying to holla at a brother— you know, some of us got it like that." Todd laughed.

"Man, your little brother sounds just like you. Poor Todd, he's brainwashed just like his brother, thinking he doesn't have to go after the women. Yeah, Trey tries to do it like that, and the brother has been single for two years," Sean said laughing.

"Hey, that's by choice, man, by choice, but as soon as I find the right one, I'm getting hitched." Trey said as he grabbed his keys.

"Well, if you really need some tips about women, Todd, just ask me and not that clown Sean. He'll have the women leaving you and laughing at you at the same time," Joe said, putting his two cents in. Everybody laughed as they walked out of the office.

♥ <u>Chapter 11</u> ♥

*I*t was Saturday morning and Trey was lying on his bed, a little baffled that he hadn't heard from Kendra. He convinced himself not to sweat it because he figured she probably didn't want to appear too anxious. Trey was a nice guy and quite the gentleman, like his father, but he was used to women falling all over him and jumping at the opportunity to be in his company. He actually liked it when a woman kept him wondering and presented more of a challenge, and being the brand new attorney that he was, he was definitely up for a challenge.

Trey always said he wanted a strong, black sister who was independent but knew how to be feminine at the same time and knew when to speak up and challenge things, but also knew how to step back and let her man take charge. Trey saw those characteristics in his mother and always said he wanted a woman just like her, but since he'd only known Kendra for a week, he knew it was certainly too early to start thinking about her being his woman. But he had to admit there was something special about her that really intrigued him. She seemed to have a certain mystery about her that he couldn't describe, but he found it to be extremely attractive.

He heard a knock on his front door, and figured it was someone from next door.

"Who is it?" he yelled.

"It's Kim."

"Come in."

Kim opened the door and yelled back to his bedroom. "Trey, what you doing? Can I come back there?"

"Come on, Kim," he yelled back.

Kim peeked in first before opening his bedroom door all the way.

"I just wanted to make sure you were decent. I don't need to be seeing any unnecessary body parts of yours." She smirked.

"Yeah right, you know you want me," Trey said, smiling as he pulled the covers over his bare chest. "And what do you want anyway? You know better than to be bothering a brother this early on a Saturday morning. And how come you're not next door cooking breakfast? You know Todd's gonna be mad if he doesn't start smelling some of your biscuits soon." They both laughed.

"You better go somewhere with that—what do I look like, a maid to you?"

"Uh yes, that's exactly what you look like, because that's who you are, the maid. So you have to do exactly what I say." Trey tried to keep a straight face.

"Yeah, okay, whatever you say, Mr. Boston. You wish you had it like that. I am not a maid. I am an assistant to Mrs. Sheila Boston, for your information, and I help out with other chores around the house. Plus your mother and father said they see me as a member of this family so that makes me your little sister. Now, how you like them apples?" Kim said, swishing her hips as she walked over to his bed. "And I don't know why you're covering up your chest. You don't have anything I want to see," she added.

"Yes I do and what do you want, girl?" Trey said, much

louder.

"Can you give me a ride to Howard County today? My car is in the shop and I don't want to ask your mother if I can take the truck."

"What's in Howard County?"

"I have some business to take care of, but it won't take long. I'll even treat you to lunch if you take me." She smiled and tilted her head.

"Girl, just admit that you want to go out with me and get it over with." He laughed.

"And what if I do want to spend some time with you? Is that a crime?"

"No, it's not a crime, but like I told you in the past, I don't want things to get out of hand with us or to mislead you. And you remember the last time we spent time together—things went way too far. But I'll take you if you promise to behave yourself," he said still laughing.

"Look, don't flatter yourself. You ain't all that, Mr. Boston, and if I didn't know any better, I would swear you were conceited."

"Yeah, okay, whatever, Kim, what time do you need to go?"

"About two o'clock."

"Okay, no problem. Now can you please get our big breakfast started so you don't upset Todd."

"Shut up boy, I'm going. I'll see you when you come next door. Oh and by the way, your chest looks good," Kim said as she walked to the bedroom door.

"Thank you. So does yours." They both laughed.

"Shut up boy," Kim said, smiling like she loved every minute of Trey's attention.

♥ ♥ ♥ ♥ ♥ ♥ ♥ ♥ ♥ ♥ ♥ ♥ ♥ ♥ ♥ ♥ ♥ ♥

After breakfast everybody went their separate ways, as was typical in the Boston household after a meal. At about 1:30 Kim went to the garage and asked Trey if he was ready to go. He'd been working on the sound system in his BMW for a while. He liked toying around with electronics and had learned most of it from Todd. The family always joked about how Todd could fix anything and could figure out how to operate all the new technologically advanced gadgets as soon as they hit the stores.

Kim and Trey were enjoying their ride to Howard County, cracking jokes and acting silly. They had about a forty-minute drive to their destination.

"So how's the job coming, Trey?" Kim asked.

"It's coming along pretty good. Not bad for my first week. I'll tell you, though, Pops threw me right into the fire my first day."

"He probably did that because he knows you can handle it. I mean, he knows you're smart, and trust me, your father is not going to give you anything that he feels you're not ready for and have you mess up his name."

"You got that right."

"I just think it's amazing that he has only lost one case in his entire twenty-year career. He is simply incredible," Kim said, shaking her head.

"Yeah, he's the man, and I just hope I can be as good as he is someday. You know? I hope I don't disappoint him."

"You won't disappointment him, Trey. You're smart and you think just like him. Just take your time, and keep learning from him, and don't be afraid to ask questions. Don't try to be perfect, like I always make the mistake of doing."

"Yeah, you're right." Trey looked over at her. "You always give good advice. You're very easy to talk to, Kim." He smiled warmly at her. And just as Kim smiled back Trey's cell phone rang.

"Hello."

"Hi Trey, this is Kendra."

"Hey, how are you doing, Kendra?"

"I'm fine, and you?"

"Oh, I'm good."

"Well, I just wanted to call and say hello. I wasn't feeling very well yesterday, but I'm better now."

"I kind of thought there may have been something going on with you yesterday morning when you were so quiet in the car. But I just figured you had a lot on your mind or that you weren't really a morning person. But anyway, I'm glad you're feeling better."

Trey could see that Kim was trying to act like she wasn't paying attention to his telephone conversation, but she couldn't help herself. Even though Kim didn't want to admit it, Trey knew she was a little jealous when it came to seeing him with another woman.

"So what are you up to?" Kendra asked.

"I'm on my way to Howard County with a friend of mine to take care of a few things. What about you?"

"Oh not much, just catching up on some housework, that's all. I wanted to go to the movies later to see that new Denzel picture. I guess it depends on how tired I am after cleaning up."

"Oh yeah, I wanted to check that out too. Were you already planning to go with someone?" Trey asked.

"No, actually I was hoping that you hadn't already seen it, so we could go together." Kendra replied.

"Oh, I see, you're trying to ask a brother out on the sly." He said, laughing.

"Sure Trey, you caught me, that's exactly what I'm doing. So how about I just come right out with it. Trey, would you like to go to the movies with me?" Trey could almost hear her smiling over the phone.

"Uh, I don't know, I need to check my schedule for tonight and get back to you," Trey said, trying his best to sound serious.

"I'm just kidding, Kendra. Sure we can check out the movie. Can you find out the times and everything and call me back and let me know what time I should pick you up?"

"Okay, I'll call you back," she said.

When Trey hung up the phone he glanced over at Kim.

"So which hot mama are you going out with tonight?" she asked.

"Hey, hey, watch your mouth. I don't go out with hot mamas, I go out with ladies. Wait a minute, that's not exactly true. I did go out with one hot mama before. If I remember correctly, her name was Kim. In fact, she looked like you. Wait a minute, it *was* you." Trey laughed.

Kim reached over and punched him on his arm.

"Right turn ahead," The female voice from Trey's GPS instructed. Trey made the right-hand turn, then looked at Kim.

"So where are we going anyway?" he asked.

"What do you mean, where are we going? I gave you the address."

"Well, I know that, but I mean what's at that location?"

"Oh, it's one of the hospitals where I might be doing my clinical trials as a nursing student."

"Oh that's cool. But wait a minute, you're going to be in school full time, doing an internship, or clinical trials as you put it, working for my mom at her spa, *and* playing housekeeper at our house? Who do you think you are, superwoman?"

"Sometimes I feel like superwoman, but I know you're not talking. If I recall, you just wrapped up a very hectic schedule yourself. You were in law school full time, working as a paralegal at your father's law firm full time, and playing on a basketball team several times a week, so I guess you thought you were Superman." They both laughed.

"Trey, you are something else. I sometimes think about that

special night you and I shared and wonder if it meant anything to you." Kim turned to look at him just as he stopped the car at a red light.

"Wow! Where did that come from, Kim? he asked as he turned to look at her.

Their eyes locked and both of them seemed to be at a loss for words.

Honk! Honk! They were both a little startled when the man in the car behind them hit his horn because the light had turned green. Trey broke his gaze with Kim and pulled off.

Once they arrived at the hospital, Kim and Trey were escorted around by one of the coordinators of the nursing program. They stayed there for about forty-five minutes, then thanked the lady and left. As they drove back toward the highway, Trey noticed a BMW dealership and asked Kim if she had time to stop so he could take a look at a vehicle. Kim said she was free for the rest of the day, so he could stop wherever he wanted. He pulled into the parking lot.

"Why are you looking at BMWs when you already have a BMW?" she asked.

"I'm trying to graduate, baby. I'm about to break out with the new 650i convertible, my dear, and it's a beast."

"I don't see anything wrong with this car. It's beautiful," Kim said. Trey owned a black 550i BMW with dark tinted windows, a GPS system, and a bumping sound system.

He circled around the parking lot, then spotted the convertible with the top dropped on display.

"Um-huh-um, look at that!" he said. "Come on, let's see if we can take it for a test drive."

"Okay," she said, getting exciting as she looked at the car. They went inside the dealership. Trey talked to a salesman for a few moments and set up the test drive. They walked outside to the shiny black convertible.

"Here we are, folks. I'll sit in the back so your girlfriend can sit up front with you," the salesman said. Trey and Kim just looked at each other and giggled.

Trey felt like he was in heaven in that car. He loved it. "I'm gonna be the man in this," he said, smiling. The other two laughed.

"I thought you already were the man, Superman, remember?" Kim said.

"Hmm, this conversation could get interesting," the salesman said. All three of them laughed.

Trey's phone rang. It was Kendra calling him back. He answered. "Hey Kendra, what's up?"

"Hi, I was calling back to tell you the movie times."

"Okay, go ahead. What are the times?" Trey asked.

"Well, it's playing at Owings Mills at 7:30 and 10:00 and it's playing in Columbia at 8:00 and 10:30, so which time would you like to go?" she asked.

"Uh, Kendra, look here, I'm sorry but I'm in the middle of something right now. Can I give you a call back in a few minutes?"

"Sure," Kendra replied, sounding a little surprised.

Trey was excited after that test drive. He went back inside the dealership to talk to the salesman and had to fight with himself to keep from buying the car. After about an hour, he walked out without the car.

"I'm glad you didn't buy that car. You have to take your time with big purchases like that," Kim said.

"So who are you, my mom now?" He put his arm around her and pulled her close to him.

"No, I'm not your mother. I just don't want to see you buy that expensive car on the fly, especially since you told me a couple of weeks ago that you were thinking about buying a house."

"Yeah you're right. Thanks for speaking up in there," Trey said.

As they drove back from Howard County, Kim looked over

at Trey.

"Aren't you forgetting something?" she asked.

"What?"

"Didn't you tell someone named Kendra that you'd call her back?"

"My goodness, you all up in my conversation, all in my business," Trey said laughing, "but thanks for reminding me. I got so caught up into that car that I forgot all about it."

Trey hit the button on his cell phone to return Kendra's call.

"Hello."

"Hey Kendra, this is Trey."

"Hi Trey."

"Alright, so you said the movie starts at about 7 and 10 at Owings Mills and Columbia right?"

"Yeah, something like that," she replied.

"Alright let's do Owings Mills, since we can have dinner in there," he said.

"Okay, sounds good. Are you picking me up?"

"Yeah, I'll pick you up at about 8 and we'll do the one that starts around 10. It's that cool?"

"Sounds good, I'll see you then."

Trey hung up the phone and looked at Kim.

"So what are you doing tonight?" he asked.

"You ask me what I'm doing tonight after you make plans with somebody else?"

"Girl, you better stop trippin', I only asked because I was curious."

"Well, I don't have anything planned for tonight. I'm just going to go back to your parents' house, finish up some laundry, and then see if Todd can give me a ride home."

"How come you're not seeing anyone, Kim? You're an attractive woman, and a really good woman."

"I haven't met anyone I'm interested in, and I don't want to go out with just anybody. I want to wait for someone special."

"I can understand that."

When they arrived back at the Boston house, Kim hugged Trey and thanked him for taking her to visit the hospital. She unlocked the front door and was surprised that he was walking in behind her.

"Don't you have to get ready for your date?" she asked, clearly happy that he was coming in with her.

"I have time. So, it doesn't look like Todd is here, do you want me to take you to your apartment?" he asked.

"No, I really need to get some stuff done around here and then I'm going to watch some of my favorite Tyler Perry plays. I can watch those DVDs over and over again and still laugh like it's my first time. I tell you, Tyler Perry is so talented and I just love Madea." She laughed.

"Plus, I love the fact that there's so much inspiration in his stories. So you go on out and have a good time. I'm going to stay here and have me a Tyler Perry and Madea night, so you know I'm going to have me a good ol' time." Kim smiled as she went to the sink to wash her hands.

"Alright, well enjoy your Tyler Perry night. How are you going to get home later?" Trey asked.

"I don't know, maybe I'll wait for you to get home from your date," she said, smiling.

"I might be out late."

"Well, maybe I'll just sleep here at your parents' house."

Trey walked over to the refrigerator and took out a bottle of water. He was thinking that he'd really had a nice time with Kim and enjoyed her company but then he thought how he was really looking forward to his date with Kendra because he was starting to like her.

"Well look Kim, I'm going to get going, so I'll talk to you later. Are you sure you're okay?"

"Yes, Trey, I'm fine. Now go and have a good time," she said as she pushed him towards the front door.

♥ <u>Chapter 12</u> ♥

$\mathcal{T}$rey arrived at Kendra's apartment and knocked on the door. She opened the door looking as fly as ever. She was dressed in a pair of dark denim, skinny jeans, a yellow silk blouse that slightly dropped off one shoulder, and high-heeled tan sandals.

"Hello, Mr. Boston."

"Hello, Miss uh…" Trey stood there, at a loss for words. Kendra gave him a look like, *Don't play with me.*

"Have you forgotten my name, or do you have so many women that you're trying to be careful not to call me the wrong one?" she asked, throwing him the same skeptical look.

"Oh, I know your name, your first name at least. But I was trying to call you by your last name when I realized that I don't know it."

"Come in, Trey," Kendra said, opening the door.

"So what is your last name?" he asked as he walked in.

"My last name? It's, um, Jackson. Miss Jackson if you're nasty."

"Oh, I don't think you wanna go there," he said, laughing. But anyway Miss Kendra Jackson, you have a nice place here, very cozy." He walked over to a painting on the wall. "This is nice, is it a Picasso?" he asked, turning to watch as she walked by in her jeans.

"Yeah right, a Picasso on whose money?" Kim went into the kitchen, finished her glass of water and headed for the door. "I'm ready Mr. Boston," she said, a flirtatious look on her face.

Trey took the opportunity to check her out from head to toe. *Um-huh-um,* he thought to himself, *she is just too fine.*

"Alright, let's hit it," he said, trying to pretend to be cool, when he really wanted a kiss.

They walked outside and Trey opened the passenger door so she could get in. He got in and selected a Maxwell CD to play before pulling off.

"So how was your day?" Kendra asked.

"It was cool. I drove the new BMW 650i convertible earlier and fell in love with it. I had to force myself to walk away from the dealership and not sign on the dotted line," he said, shaking his head, "because that car was sweet, almost as sweet as you."

"Oh really? Trey, I must say you sure know how to make a woman feel good. I mean comparing me to a car, now that's what I call a man who knows exactly the right thing to say to a woman." She laughed before continuing. "And what's wrong with the BMW you already have? This is a beautiful car, plus I love the television screens and all the other gadgets you got in here."

"Yeah, my little brother, Todd, put most of this stuff in here. He's like a technological genius, it's amazing. He can figure anything out—how to bypass this and reconfigure that. The boy is bad." Trey smiled.

"How old is he?"

"Seventeen, just graduated from high school and got accepted into Morehouse in Atlanta. He's a good guy. I'm really proud of him, you know."

"Ah, that's great. Sounds like you two are pretty close."

"Yeah, we're twelve years apart, but we're very close, that's my buddy. My mom always says we're both just like my dad. She says we act just like him, enjoy the same things, and have a whole bunch of his habits." Trey smiled.

"Do you have any other brothers or sisters?"

"Nope, it's just me and Todd. What about you? Do you have any brothers or sisters?"

"No, I'm an only child. My mom probably wanted more, but she was killed in a car accident when I was younger and then my father moved away. He allowed me to stay here with my aunt," Kendra said, not making eye contact.

"Were you lonely growing up?"

"No, I was really close to my mom and we did a lot of things together. Then when she died I went to live with my aunt, who had three girls and a boy, so they were like my brother and sisters."

Kendra quickly changed the subject. It was obvious she was uncomfortable talking about her past and her family. "So this car is a stick shift. I wish I knew how to drive a stick," she said.

Trey was kind of surprised at how abruptly she switched subjects, but he didn't comment on it. "You want me to teach you how to drive a stick?" he asked.

"Sure, would you do that?" She sounded excited.

"Yeah, I don't mind. But I'm not going to teach you in this car. I have another little car, a Honda, that I can teach you in, 'cause I can't let you strip the gears in my baby."

"Oh, okay. I don't care what I learn in, I just want to learn. Is it hard?"

"No, not all. You're already a good driver, hopefully," he said, laughing, "and driving a stick is all about coordination. You're a smart girl, so it'll probably take you just a couple of hours to learn."

"A couple of hours! Really? I don't know about that." She

laughed.

The movie they saw was a thriller-type flick. It was making Kendra a little edgy, so Trey put his arm around her. During certain scenes she even grabbed on to him which he enjoyed. At one point Trey leaned over and kissed her on the cheek. She turned to face him and their lips met. As they shared a kiss, Kendra began touching his face—until she came to her senses and abruptly stopped. She suddenly felt she was moving too fast and didn't know if she planned to continue dating Trey. She knew she had met him under false pretenses, trying to please her father, and she didn't want to lead him on or get her own feelings all wrapped up. She could tell he was a nice guy. Plus, she didn't want to take things too far, because she knew she was attracted to him and she didn't want to take a chance on being tempted to commit fornication. She was determined to live a life that was pleasing to God. She figured the sooner she got out of this with Trey, the better it would be for everyone, even though her own father told her to use her womanly wiles to destroy the Boston family. Kendra knew she was nothing like her father. All she wanted was a normal life, and to move past her family's tragic past.

When the movie was over, Trey told Kendra he was going to take her home. It was getting late and he had to turn in early. He'd promised his mom that he would go to church with the rest of the family the next day.

"Are you going to church tomorrow?" he asked.

"Yes, I am. I try not to let anything make me miss church. I just started going back not too long ago. I hadn't been in years after my mom died. It just seemed like my life started to unravel when that happened, and even though church was the very place that I needed to be, it was the very place that I stayed away from. I probably could have healed a lot better and sooner had I continued to go to church. But going to church just made me miss my mother so much. She used to take me with her every Sunday. She loved church, and I think that's what made me stay away so long. It just didn't seem the same sitting in there without her. But during the years I stayed away, I felt like there was such a void in my life. I thought it was because my mom was gone, but it was more than that—it was the fact that I was not nurturing my close relationship with God. So I found a really nice church about ten months ago and joined, and I've been going ever since." She smiled.

"That's good, my dad has always gone to church with us. That's how I want to be with my wife and kids. I think that's so important and really needed in more families. The man needs to take the lead as the head of the family and really set good examples for his children to follow, you know. That's what my dad taught us." Trey pulled into Kendra's apartment complex. He looked over at her. She was suddenly very quiet and looked sad. "Would you like to go to church with me tomorrow, Kendra?" he asked. He caught her off guard with that question.

"Uh well, um, I guess so. I mean, I don't have to sing on the choir tomorrow, so yeah, I'll go with you," she said, smiling, then she realized what she'd just done. Here she was agreeing to go to church with him, when she needed to be pulling away. "Sing on the choir, now see, that's the kind of woman I like, a good-looking woman who sings on the choir" Trey said smiling. Kendra smiled back. "But seriously, I'm glad you're going to church with us. My family is nice. Trust me, you'll like them. We'll be going to the eleven o'clock service, so I'll pick you up at nine thirty. Is that cool?" he asked.

"That's fine. I'll be ready," she said.

When Kendra walked inside her apartment, she felt disappointed that she had agreed to go to church with the Boston family. After all, she wanted to pull back from Trey and tell her father that she couldn't get close to him because he wasn't interested in her, so he could forget about his stupid plan of revenge on the Boston family and she could get on with her life. Now she had to sit in church with the family, and she just didn't feel right about it. She had a good heart and was a good person, and she knew that Trey was a great guy. He didn't deserve this.

♥ <u>Chapter 13</u> ♥

*K*endra looked like an angel walking into the church with Trey. She had on an off-white, ankle-length dress with lace trim, high heels, and her hair was swept up. Trey was handsomely dressed in an olive-colored suit with a nice tie, and nice shoes. They looked like the perfect couple.

Mr. and Mrs. Boston walked in with Todd and Kim. Trey didn't know Kim was coming with them. The family spotted Trey and walked over to him and Kendra. Trey hugged his mom and said hello to everyone.

"Mom, Dad this is my friend Kendra," Trey said.

"Hello, Mr. and Mrs. Boston, it's a pleasure to meet you," Kendra said, smiling.

"It's nice to meet you too, Kendra," Mrs. Boston said.

"Good to meet you, young lady," Tony said.

Trey then introduced Kendra to Todd and Kim.

"Hi, Todd. I hear you were accepted into college, congratulations. Your brother speaks highly of you, and I hear Morehouse is a great school." Kendra shook Todd's hand.

"Thank you. It's nice to meet you, Kendra," Todd said. He gave Trey the eye, like *Wow, she's bad.* Tony came and stood at the end of the pew motioning everyone inside. Trey went in first, followed by Kendra, Todd, and Kim; then Mrs. Boston and Tony sat on the end. Trey was hoping Kim's feelings weren't hurt because he had a date. Even though he wasn't interested in a relationship with Kim, he still cared about her feelings. It was a special day in church because the pastor was going to pray for Todd and other teenagers who were about to go to college.

During the service, Trey had his hand on his knee and Kendra slipped her hand underneath his. Trey could tell she was a "touchy-feely" kind of person, and he didn't mind a bit—in fact, he was used to that type of nurturing from a woman. His mother was that way.

Ironically the sermon was titled Choosing Your Path, and was about what people should do when they feel they've come to a point in their life when they have to make a decision to do the right thing or something they know is wrong. The pastor's message was clear that the Bible calls for us to choose the right path and to acknowledge God in all our ways and that He will direct our paths.

Everyone was very much into the service, but Kendra was feeling it in a different way. It was as if God had the pastor preach that sermon directly to her, because everything that she was going through with her father was related to doing right or wrong. Kendra tried desperately to fight back the tears that were filling up inside her eyes, but she knew she'd lost the battle when she felt one roll down her cheek. It was on the left side of her face, where Todd was sitting, and since he was leaning over on Kim, he never even noticed.

Kendra silently prayed to Jesus that He would help her as she wanted to choose the right thing but she didn't want to hurt her father or have him think that she was abandoning or disobeying him. She knew that it would take Divine intervention to get her out of having to do something bad to the Boston family and to still have her Dad love her. After all, he was all she had and she was certainly all he had.

Kendra was able to pull herself together by the end of the service, and it was a good thing because the pastor called the Boston family and several other families up to the front for prayer for Todd and the other teens. Each week the church prayed for several college-bound kids at a time, and this week it was Todd's turn. The Boston family went up to the front. Kendra wanted to stay seated, but Trey motioned for her to come along. She felt a little nervous because she was not a part of the family, not even close. As the pastor prayed for the students, everyone in the church held hands and bowed their heads.

When church was over, Sheila Boston told the family that she and Tony were taking everyone on a dinner cruise down the inner harbor and that they were making it a family day. Trey looked at Kendra to try and gauge her reaction but really couldn't, so he just asked her if she wanted to go. Kendra said she was game, so they got into Trey's car and followed Tony since everyone else was riding with him.

Once they were all settled on the boat, Tony started making conversation with Kendra.

"So I understand you're about to start law school, young lady."

"Yes, I am, and I'm really looking forward to it," she replied.

"Now, is this something my son talked you into, or did you already have plans to become a lawyer before you met him?" Everyone laughed.

"No sir, I already had plans before I met him," Kendra said, laughing as well.

"Okay, I was just checking, because the Boston men can be quite persuasive, you know. We do it for a living."

Sheila jumped in. "Don't pay my husband any attention, he always has something to say. So where are you from, Kendra?"

"I'm from Maryland. I grew up in Pikesville and now I have an apartment in Towson," she replied.

Trey changed the subject. He suspected someone would soon start asking questions about her family or her parents, and he did not want to put her on the spot or make her sad.

"So Mom, are you going to cry when Todd leaves for school?" Trey asked, smiling.

"No, not at all. What makes you think I'm going to cry? I didn't cry when you left, did I?" Sheila said as everyone at the table broke out in laughter.

"Come on, Ma, you cried at the house before we drove down to Atlanta, cried once we got to Atlanta, and then cried when you and Dad were leaving Atlanta," Trey said.

Tony chimed in. "Yeah, it was tough dragging this cry baby around for an entire weekend. Everywhere we went the tears poured out. I tried to take her to a restaurant for dinner, and she started crying in the restaurant. I took her to a nice hotel in downtown Atlanta and tried to get romantic to take her mind off Trey, and she started crying right in the middle of the romance session. Y'all don't need anymore details than that—that's grown, married folks business," he said, laughing. "Then that Sunday morning we went to Ebenezer Baptist Church, home of the Reverend Dr. Martin Luther King, Jr., and she really broke down in there. It was tough, I tell you." Tony rubbed Sheila's shoulders. "But she's my baby; she can cry all she wants to over those big boys of ours. To tell you the truth, I was crying too— crying for joy that Trey was gone and we had a break for a while," Tony joined in on the laughter he was causing.

Kim was laughing and having a good time and didn't seem to mind that Trey was there with a date. She was friendly toward Kendra and they even went to the restroom together, which is a sure sign that women are getting along with one another.

When the three-hour cruise was over, everyone said goodbye to Trey and told Kendra that it was a pleasure meeting her. Sheila even invited her to her spa for a free day of pampering, and Kendra gladly accepted.

♥ ♥ ♥ ♥ ♥ ♥ ♥ ♥ ♥ ♥ ♥ ♥ ♥ ♥ ♥ ♥ ♥ ♥ ♥

It was about 8 o'clock when Trey took Kendra back to her apartment. She invited him in.

"Trey, thanks so much for a wonderful day and a wonderful week. You have a great family. I guess that explains why you're such a great guy," Kendra said as she sat next to him on the couch.

"You're quite welcome, and thank you for a nice week as well. I must say I have really enjoyed your company," Trey said. "Can I ask you something?"

"Sure."

"Why don't you have a man? I mean, you already told me you were single and not dating anyone, but why? Somebody as fine and sweet as you are should have men knocking her door down," Trey said, looking Kendra over.

"I told you, I was too busy with school, work, and church to be in a relationship. Besides, the right man hasn't come along. No, I should say God hasn't sent the right man along yet so I've just been concentrating on me and the Lord. And you're asking me why am I single—I should be asking you. You're handsome, smooth, charming, charismatic, intelligent, and a lot of fun to be with. How come you don't have women fighting over you?"

"Well, to tell you the truth, I do have a lot of women fighting over me, but I just let them go at it. Then when I get sick of them, I tell them to beat it," Trey said, laughing. "No, the truth is I was in a relationship with someone I really cared about for two years, and we started having problems and scheduling conflicts, and then just grew apart and stopped making time for each other all together. It hurt, but we finally realized that it wasn't meant to be and called it quits."

"So have you dated anyone since?" she asked.

"No, not seriously. Just a date here and there. I don't like to lead people on. I'm very careful about how I treat women when I'm in their company so as not to send the wrong message. But sometimes no matter how hard you try to be careful, someone catches feelings when they shouldn't, you know what I mean?" He looked at Kendra.

"What, are you trying to give me a hint, Mr. Boston?"

"Oh no, not at all, Miss Jackson, you're cool with me." They both laughed.

Kendra turned on the television, and saw that the movie *Boomerang* was on.

"Oh my goodness, I haven't seen this movie in a long time. It's one of my favorites," she said.

"You've got to be kidding me," said Trey. "I love this movie too. Eddie Murphy is my dawg."

Kendra moved over and snuggled up next to Trey. He gently caressed her shoulder and arm as they watched the movie. Fortunately, the movie had just started. Trey and Kendra shared a few kisses, but didn't take it any further than that. It was almost as if they both knew there was a line that they weren't going to cross, even though the words had not been spoken.

After the movie was over, Kendra sat up. "Look, it's getting late, and I have to get up early in the morning, so we should call it a night," she said, looking at Trey.

He felt like a little boy when she said that, but he played it off because he didn't want to show how much he wanted to stay, not Mr. Cool.

"Alright, baby, I guess I should get going then," he said, straightening his clothes as he stood up. Kendra walked him to the door and they shared one more kiss before he left.

As Trey walked away, Kendra shut the door and leaned against it, trying to catch her breath. *Woo, this man is all that and a scoop of ice cream,* she thought. *I'd better get out of this real soon before somebody gets hurt.*

♥ _Chapter 14_ ♥

"*L*ights out," one of the prison guards yelled through the cell block. Rob was so disappointed that the day had ended and his daughter Kendra had not come to see him for her usual Sunday visit. He was concerned because she was so upset when she left him a couple of days ago, but she promised she would come back on Sunday for her usual visit.

"Man, I don't know, Wayne, something's goin' on with my baby girl. It's not like her to miss her Sunday visit. I mean, come on man, we've been cellmates for just about the entire time we've been in here, and have you ever known Kendra to miss a visit?" Rob asked.

"As a matter of fact, she's never missed a Sunday that I can remember. What do you think is wrong?" Wayne asked.

"I have no idea. I tried calling her tonight and she didn't answer. Man, I hope I didn't push her away by being too forceful, you know? She's all I got. You know how it is being in here and your family's out there; you don't wanna lose them, you don't want them to forget about you. I don't know what I'd do without my baby girl," Rob said, clearly upset.

"Well, man, what happened when she was here the other

day? Did you all get into it or what?"

"No, not exactly. See, I've been asking Kendra to help me take care of something for a while now, and she was on board with everything until she came here on Friday talking crazy like she didn't wanna do it and how it was wrong and all this other crap. So, you know, I jumped on her case and told her that she owed it to me to help me out and that it couldn't wait until I get released, that I wanted it done now. The whole time she was just talking like a completely different person, you know. Like somebody had been able to get inside her head and turn her against her old man, and you know I don't like that," Rob said angrily.

"Who do you think it is?" Wayne asked, pretending that he hadn't overheard Rob and Kendra's conversation the other day.

"It's not who I think it is, it's who I know it is—that damn Boston family, that's who." Rob reached over to turn his lamp on.

"The Boston family, as in Tony Boston, the bastard who put me in here, and his son, that's who it is." he looked furious.

Wayne was Rob's friend, but deep down inside he thought Rob was really guilty of raping his student because of some of the things he'd said throughout the years, and Wayne thought he had some nerve hating Tony Boston and blaming the fact that he was in jail on him when he was probably guilty.

"Man, how in the world did the Boston family get to Kendra? What business would they have talking to her? How do they even know who she is?" Wayne asked.

"It's a long story. You know how I always told you I was going to make Tony Boston pay for what he did to me? Well, I asked Kendra to help me. See, I read in the paper that his son Trey had passed the bar exam and was joining his father's law firm. So I told Kendra to find a way to meet Trey and get in good with him and then find a way to destroy them. I told her to make it seem like Tony tried to come on to her and make his wife think he's messing around—anything to take those bastards down."

"Rob, tell me you're not serious. Tell me you didn't ask Kendra to do that."

"Yes, I did too! Look, I was in the prime of my life, a good life too, when the man who was supposed to be my friend turned on me. He was supposed to be so upright and morally correct—he's full of crap, that's what he is, and I want my baby girl to drop those bastards to their knees so Tony Boston can see what it feels like to lose his wife, his kid, and his livelihood, just like I did," Rob said, now with a faraway stare-almost scary.

"I know you wanna get back at him and everything, but you shouldn't involve Kendra. She's innocent in all this and she could really get hurt. Besides, man, she's been through a lot already. You sure you want her to go through with this?" Wayne asked, with a concerned look on his face.

"Look, you let me worry about all of that, that's my baby girl, my blood. She's gonna do what I tell her to do." Rob turned out the lamp.

♥ Chapter 15 ♥

*I*t was almost dark when Mr. and Mrs. Boston pulled up to their house. "Nobody's home, honey, maybe we'll have a nice peaceful evening," Sheila said as she smiled at her husband.

"Yes ma'am, sounds good to me. It's about time I spent some quality one-on-one time with my beautiful wife."

"And baby, this is perfect timing because I brought some new massage oils home with me from the spa. Maybe I'll slide some all over your body tonight," she said as he helped her out of the car.

"Oh yes, Mrs. Boston, now you're speaking my language."

They went inside. Sheila walked upstairs and started running a nice hot tub of water in the Jacuzzi.

After about ten minutes, she yelled downstairs to Tony, "Babe, would you like to take a bath with me?"

"Sure, that sounds good, baby. I'm coming up now," Tony said as he walked up the stairs.

"Alright, hurry up dear, the water's nice and hot like you like it, the bubbles are bubbling, the candles are lit, and your wife is in the mood for some good ol' loving."

"I heard that," Tony said as he walked into the bathroom and grabbed his wife around her waist, pulling her close to him.

He looked into her eyes. "I love you, Mrs. Boston."

"I love you too, Mr. Boston."

"I'm glad we're alone tonight, because that dress is turning me on. Now turn around and let me take it off of you—or should I say peel it off, since it's a little tight."

"Excuse me!" Sheila said as she turned around and sent a piercing stare at Tony.

"No, baby, it's tight in a good way, in all the right places, showing all the right things. I like it when you dress like that sometimes."

"Uh huh, don't try to fix it up now." She turned back around so he could take it off for her.

Tony unzipped her dress down the back and started biting her shoulders as they were revealed. Sheila had a beautiful body for a middle-aged woman. He started unsnapping her bra and heard her giggle.

"What, am I too rough?

"No, not at all." She turned around and grabbed his hands. "I'm laughing because I'm thinking about the very first time we made love, and how you struggled so hard trying to get my bra off. It was the funniest thing. I felt so sorry for you, because you were so nervous and so anxious, but you just couldn't get those snaps to cooperate."

"Yeah, okay, okay, real funny. It was your fault, with all that moaning and groaning, 'Oh Tony, oh Tony, I love your hands, oh Tony, you have such a nice touch, oh Tony.' I said to myself, *If she doesn't shut up with all that noise...*" They both laughed hysterically.

"Tony, you are so full of it. And you still owe me some money for my bra that you destroyed."

"Yeah right, you made me destroy it because you wanted me so bad. Now turn around, let me see how fast I can get this bra off now."

"Sure Tony," she said giggling.

Within a few moments they were both in the Jacuzzi enjoying the hot bubble bath and each other.

♥ <u>Chapter 16</u> ♥

Over the next few months Kendra and Trey continued to spend time together on dates, and fun ones at that. He took her places like roller skating and horseback riding and was about to take her parachuting but she got scared and backed out. Trey was quite the gentleman, and Kendra knew that she was falling for him big time. Kendra had tried to bring herself to call it quits with Trey so many times, but realized that she enjoyed being with him so much. Now she was concentrating on finding a way to be honest with him about her father, hoping that Trey would understand and forgive her.

She was getting in good with his family as well. She had been over to their house on quite a few occasions and even rode to Atlanta with them when they dropped Todd off for school. Even though she was having a lot of fun and feeling good about life for the first time in years, she still couldn't forget about her father sitting in prison for a crime he said he didn't commit. No matter how much she had fallen for Trey and enjoyed the attention from the Boston family, she couldn't stop thinking about her own family. She wished Tony Boston would have won her dad's case like he did with all the rest of his cases, so that their lives could have been much better and she could still have her mom.

Even though Kendra went to church and sang in the choir, she struggled with forgiveness in that area, but she felt like she couldn't talk to anyone about it. She loved her father dearly, but she questioned whether he was truly innocent—or if he raped his student? Kendra had to know the truth.

She wanted to meet the young lady who'd accused her Dad of rape but wondered how she was going to find her. Then she realized that all the information was probably in her father's file at Boston & Associates. She hoped it was still there. It would contain information about the trial, the police report, and the victim's identity. She would somehow have to sneak into the file room and find it.

When Kendra left work, she went home and looked through the newspaper articles she'd saved to find the exact date when her father was accused of rape, when his trial started, and when he was sentenced to jail. She didn't know how the files were sorted at the firm, so she wanted to make sure she had as much information with her as possible. Kendra called Trey to find out how late he was going to be at the office. She pretended she wanted to come over to his house and watch a movie and wanted to know what time he would be getting off. Trey told Kendra he would be leaving the office at about six that night, and she agreed to meet him at his house at eight.

Kendra pulled up to Boston & Associates at about six-thirty. She saw that Trey's car was gone but noticed several other cars were still there. This was actually a good thing, since Trey had introduced her to many of the office employees and someone was bound to let her in. Kendra knocked on the door. The cleaning lady happened to be in the front lobby and could see Kendra through the glass. She came to the door.

"Hi sweetie," she said as she opened the door and let Kendra in.

"Hello," Kendra said. She was so nervous she couldn't remember the older woman's name. "I hope I didn't miss Trey. I'm just going to go up to his office." Kendra walked over to the elevator.

"Okay baby." The lady hardly paid any attention to Kendra.

She found her way to the file room, and after about twenty minutes she found her father's file. Kendra spent a few minutes reading some of the details of the trial and the witness' testimony. Tears welled up in her eyes as she read how the victim accused her father of pretending he needed help with a project that he was working on for an upcoming school event and asked if she could meet him in his office later that evening. The victim said she thought Mr. Stewart was one of the nicest people she'd ever met because he was always ready to lend a helping hand to his students. She then explained that she felt dizzy after drinking a drink that Mr. Stewart fixed for her and that he later forced himself on her. Kendra then heard the elevator bell and quickly wrote down the victim's name and information. As she closed the file, a picture fell out. She took it with her, assuming it was a picture of the victim. She quietly left the file room and headed to the elevator. When the elevator door opened, the same cleaning lady was getting off and Kendra smiled, trying not to look upset.

"Good night," Kendra said.

"Goodnight, sweetie," the woman replied.

Kendra pulled up to Trey's house at about eight-thirty. He wasn't in his part of the house, so she figured he was next door. Kim happened to be there and opened the door for her.

"Hello, Kendra," Kim said.

"Hi Kim, how are you?"

"I'm fine, thanks, how are you?"

"I'm great. Is Trey here?"

"Yes, he's here. I'll get him for you."

Kendra walked into the living room and took a seat. She felt like she was carrying the entire world on her shoulders and was on the verge of tears. Plus it didn't help that Kim was obviously alone in the house with Trey. Kendra knew that Kim clearly had a thing for Trey, and she believed Trey had some feelings for Kim as well. She had never asked whether the two of them had a history together because deep down inside she really didn't want to know the answer.

Trey came downstairs wearing some sweats and a tank top. He kissed Kendra on the lips and told her he was upstairs hooking up the surround sound on the new plasma TV in his parents' bedroom. They then headed over to his place. "How was your day?" he asked.

"Pretty good, and yours?"

"Busy. We have a lot of new cases coming in so we're swamped. But in the true Boston spirit, I intend to win all my cases." Trey smiled.

"What if you don't win all your cases? What if you lose one like your father did—how will you feel?" Kendra hoped this would prompt him to talk about the case his father lost.

"No one's perfect, baby. If I lose one, I just lose one."

"So what happened to make your father lose that case? What kind of case was it?"

"It was a rape case, and the man accused was a guy my father went to college with. They lost touch for a while after school, and when my father heard from him again, he'd become a college professor and was accused of raping one of his students. It was a big mess, and my father took the case personally because he'd been close to the guy in college. In fact, the guy took my mother out on a date before she started dating my father. The guy used to joke with my father, saying my father stole my mother away from him.

"But anyway, when the case came up, there was just so much evidence against him it was crazy, and his own wife thought he was guilty. But she was such a good woman, she tried to stick by him."

Kendra's eyes opened wide at that point.

Trey continued. "Anyway, my father said it was a very difficult case, and when the witness took the stand she gave convincing testimony, and then other female students started coming forward saying that he had come on to them, and the prosecution said they had evidence that he'd slept with other students but that it was consensual and they were over the age of eighteen." They walked in Trey's place and he headed for the refrigerator. "You want something to drink, baby?" he asked.

"Yeah, just some water, please, and I need to use the bathroom." Kendra quickly turned her face so he couldn't see the tears about to fall from her eyes. Once inside the bathroom, she grabbed a towel and smashed it up to her face trying to silence her cry. She realized now why her mother was so upset when she drove away from the courthouse that day. She also realized why she used to hear her parents arguing over her father's frequent late nights. She was more determined than ever to find out the truth.

Kendra got herself together and went back and sat on the sofa. She was glad Trey had turned the lights down and was about to start the movie. Trey was tired and fell asleep almost as soon as the movie started. For the rest of the night Kendra thought about nothing but her mother and what she must have gone through.

♥ Chapter 17 ♥

Trey was sitting at work when Joe and Sean walked into his office.

"Whassup, you ready to go to this game or what?" Sean asked.

"Aww man, I lost track of time," Trey said as he glanced at his watch. "Let me change real quick and we can get out of here. I was hoping I would've heard from my girl by now. I don't know what's going on. I've been trying to reach her since last night." Trey walked to the closet to get his jeans and a shirt.

"She's probably mad because you're going to the game tonight with the fellas. You know how women get when they start wanting all of your time," Joe said.

"Yeah, and it's about time you started hanging out with us a little more. That girl got you wrapped around her finger, man, you don't even hang out with your boys no more. What's up with that?" Sean said, shrugging his shoulders. "I mean, she's fine and everything, but we've been boys for years."

Joe cut in. "Look, as fine as she is, I'd be all up under her too, you know what I'm saying. I mean, you got to make sure that don't get away from you because, man, from everything you say about her, she sounds like the kind of woman you need to marry."

"Sure is," Trey said.

"Oh no, I was just joking, man. Boy, you really are wrapped around her finger," Joe said. Everybody laughed.

The three of them didn't notice the cleaning lady, Miss Gertrude, standing in the doorway. She was a retired teacher who liked to keep busy, so she cleaned the office three times a week. She asked Tony for the job five years ago because she said she was bored sitting at home and it was her way of thanking him for representing her son per bono.

"Oh, hey, Miss Gerty," Trey said when he saw her at the door.

"Hi there baby, how you young men doing?" she asked.

"Fine," they all said in unison.

"I hear you boys in here having a serious conversation. I didn't mean to disturb your man talk." She smiled.

The guys laughed.

"That's okay, Miss Gerty," Trey said.

"Yeah, that's okay, Miss Gerty, we're just trying to talk some sense into Trey about moving too fast with this new lady in his life," Joe said.

"You mean that pretty young lady who works at your parents' house? Because your mom told me that she thought you two had a thing for each other months ago," Miss Gerty said.

"Oh no, she's talking about Kim," Trey said. He smiled at his boys. "No, this is my new girlfriend Kendra. Here's a picture of her."

"Oh, her. She's beautiful, and she works here doesn't she?"

"No, she doesn't," Trey answered.

"Well, I saw her in here the other night. I think she was in the file room—that's the floor she was on," Miss Gerty said with a puzzled look on her face.

"No, Miss Gerty, I think you're mistaken. Kendra wouldn't

DESIRES OF THE HEART

have any business in the file room. You probably saw her in my office a couple of times with me," Trey said, dismissing Miss Gerty's comments.

"Now look sweetie, Miss Gerty might be getting old, but I got good sense and a good memory, thank the Lord, and I know what I saw. I'm telling you, I saw this young lady in the building the other night and she was upstairs on the file room floor. I didn't say anything because I figured she was an intern or something, but now I remember I've seen her in here with you too."

"Oh okay, Miss Gerty, maybe you're right. She might have been checking on something for me. Lately my father's been throwing a lot of work my way, so I probably had her go get some files for me or something like that." Trey sounded like he was trying to convince himself.

"Alright young men, I'm going to head on out of here now," she said as she emptied Trey's trash can and put it back. "Since you're working late, Trey, I'll dust your office the next time around. You boys be careful out there and have a good time."

"Okay Miss Gerty, thanks," Trey said. "Alright fellas, I just need about ten more minutes and I'll be ready to bounce."

Trey was changing his clothes but his mind was still on what Miss Gerty told him about Kendra. *What could she have been doing in the file room?*

♥ Chapter 18 ♥

Over the next few days Kendra's only mission in life was finding that rape victim. Since she was a lawyer in training, she had no trouble researching and locating people. From the looks of things, the victim, Rhonda Wallace, still had the same address she had twelve years ago.

Kendra had no idea how she was going to approach the victim, and then while surfing the Internet she found her answer. It appeared that Rhonda Wallace had a nonprofit organization that helped empower young women. Kendra decided she would pay her a visit and act like she had a family member who she thought could benefit from the organization.

When Kendra arrived at Rhonda's office, she told the secretary she had an appointment.

"Yes, I see your name right here. You may have a seat and Miss Wallace will be with you shortly," the secretary said.

Kendra had studied Rhonda's picture enough that when Rhonda came into the waiting area, she knew it was her. She still looked exactly like her picture that had fallen out of her father's file at the law office. Rhonda introduced herself and invited Kendra into her office. Kendra thanked her and once again explained why she was there.

"As I told you on the phone, I have a family member who I think may be able to benefit from your program and I wanted to know more about it." Kendra smiled at Rhonda.

They chatted for an hour, with Rhonda doing most of the talking. Rhonda explained why she started the program. She said that when she was a young college student a man whom she really believed in and trusted misused her trust and raped her. She said her program was designed to help young women who had been abused, molested, or raped and to provide counseling to young women to teach them how to avoid becoming a victim.

As Rhonda talked, Kendra thought she seemed like a sincere person who was passionate about her organization and its mission. Kendra inquired more about Rhonda's situation and how this college professor took advantage of her. Surprisingly, Rhonda opened up. She said what happened to her twelve years ago had made it very difficult for her to trust men. Rhonda told Kendra she had looked up to her professor and that he was a smart man.

"He taught me a lot and I enjoyed his class very much. I kind of suspected that he was interested in me when he called me one evening at home out of nowhere. He said he got my number from my student information card and asked me if I could help with an event he was hosting at the school. Even after I agreed to help him, he continued talking to me on the phone, asking if I had a boyfriend and other personal things. I'd heard rumors that he'd slept with some of the girls on campus, but I'd just dismissed them. I had so much respect for him, I just didn't want to believe that stuff.

"Then when I went to his office one evening to help him with the project, things took a crazy turn. We started working, and he poured me some wine, saying he wanted to celebrate because big things were about to happen for him. The wine tasted good, like it was extra sweet. It must have had some kind of mind-altering drug in it because I felt really tipsy, really fast. He started kissing me and unbuttoning my blouse. He told me he thought I was pretty and that he had been interested in me ever since the first day I walked into his classroom. I told him that I didn't feel well and that I wanted to go home, but he wouldn't let me. He started taking off my blouse and getting forceful with me. I remember I started crying and he still wouldn't stop. Then he just forced my clothes off so that he could have his way with me," Rhonda paused. She seemed to notice how much her story was affecting Kendra, despite Kendra's attempt to hide her emotions. She asked Kendra if she was okay.

"I'm sorry. It's just that I know someone who had something similar happen to them. Please excuse me," Kendra said as she wiped her tears.

"Please don't apologize. Rape is a very painful experience. I just started being able to tell that story without crying myself, and sometimes I still cry," Rhonda said.

The two talked a little longer and then said their goodbyes. Kendra thanked Rhonda and said she would have her relative call her. As Kendra left that office, there was no doubt in her mind that her father had indeed raped Rhonda Wallace.

♥ <u>Chapter 19</u> ♥

Sheila Boston had just closed up shop at her day spa and was heading to her car when her cell phone rang.

"Hello," she said.

"Hey ma, it's Todd."

Sheila smiled. "Hey sweetie, how you doing?"

"I'm fine. Our plane is about to take off now so we should be right on time. Are you still picking us up from the airport?"

"Yeah baby, I'm picking you up—but did you say picking *us* up? Is someone with you?"

"Oh yeah, Ma, I meant to tell you. I'm bringing a friend home to take to the charity ball as my date tomorrow night."

"Todd, what are you thinking? You've only been in school for a couple of months, how do you know somebody well enough to bring home to spend the night? Your father is not going to like this. And you should have talked to us about it first," Sheila said with obvious irritation.

"Come on Ma, it's not that serious. I've known her for years. We went to middle school and high school together. She goes to Spelman now, but she's from Baltimore and she's gonna stay with her own family when she comes home." Todd talked low so the girl couldn't hear him. "Plus, you know I'm not crazy. I'm not trying to have a girl spend the night in your house. I know you and Dad don't play that. Y'all taught me better than that." Todd laughed.

"Okay baby. Well, I'm on my way to the airport so I'll see you at six-thiry. Y'all have a good flight. I love you."

"Okay Ma, I love you too."

Sheila pulled up at the airport at 6:15. She parked far back, waiting for Todd to call her so she could pull up closer. In the meantime, she called her husband.

"Hello," Tony said.

"Hi Dear, I just wanted to let you know that I'm at the airport picking up Todd."

"Okay baby. I'm leaving work now, so I should be home when you two get there."

"Okay, sounds good. And let me tell you, I am so excited about tomorrow night. I can't wait for that charity ball," Sheila said.

"I know, baby, I'm excited too."

"Okay, I gotta go. Todd's beeping in, so he must be coming out of the airport. I'll see you at home. I love you."

"I love you too, baby, bye-bye."

Sheila pulled up when she spotted Todd and got of of the car. He ran over to give her a hug,

"Hey Todd, I missed my baby so much." She kissed him on the cheek.

"Hey Mom, I missed you too," he said, smiling from ear to ear. "Mom, this is Brittney, my friend from Spelman." He pointed to the young lady standing next to him.

"Hello Brittney, nice to meet you. Wow, aren't you a pretty young lady!" Sheila said, smiling at her.

"Hi Mrs. Boston, it's nice to meet you too. I've heard a lot of wonderful things about you," Brittney said, smiling back at the two of them.

"Well, come on kids, let's get this luggage and get going."

They loaded up the trunk and got into Sheila's SUV.

"So how's school, son?" Sheila asked.

"It's real cool Ma. I like Morehouse a lot."

"I told you Morehouse was perfect for you. And is this your first year at Spelman, Brittney?" Sheila asked.

"Yes ma'am."

"So how do you like it?"

"I love it, it's great," Brittney answered.

They arrived at Brittney's parents' house to drop her off, "I'll see you tomorrow night at the charity ball, Brittney," Sheila said.

"Okay, I'll see you then, Mrs. Boston," Brittney said, as she and Todd got out. Todd walked her to the door.

"Alright, I'll call you later Brittney," Todd said.

"Okay Todd, and thanks for inviting me," she said as they hugged. Brittney walked into the house.

About twenty minutes later, Todd and Sheila pulled up to their house. When Todd walked in, Kim ran over and hugged him.

"Hey there Toddy-Toddy, it's so nice to see you. I missed you so much," she said, pinching his cheek. Kim loved Todd like a little brother.

"Hey Kim, I missed you too." Todd kissed her on the cheek.

"So how do you like Morehouse?" Kim asked.

"It's nice. I'm glad I listened to Trey and my father when they told me to go there."

"Hey there, son," Tony said as he walked into the kitchen."

"Hey Pops, what's happening?" Todd walked over and gave Tony a hug.

"How's my old alma mater treating you?" Tony asked.

"Oh I'm straight. It's everything you and Trey said it would be and more."

"Cool. Well, I'm glad to have you home, son." Tony said.

"Everybody, dinner's ready," Kim yelled.

"Where's Trey?" Todd asked.

"He went to a game with the fellas. He said he'll be here later," Sheila said.

As the family ate, they talked about how excited they were about tomorrow's charity ball. Sheila told them all to come to the spa to get facials and manicures so they could look extra special. Kim told Mrs. Boston she would help out at the spa since so many extra clients from the firm were coming to get ready for the ball.

♥ Chapter 20 ♥

By 6:30 the next morning Sheila was at the Paradise Day Spa getting things ready before the wave of clients came in. It was a beautiful Saturday morning and they were expecting close to fifty people, most of them trying to get gorgeous for the charity ball that night.

Although Kim had agreed to help out, she wasn't coming in until the afternoon. One by one the hair stylists, nail technicians, and massage therapists arrived. The employees were nice and professional and the atmosphere was always relaxing and positive. Sheila made sure that she screened her employees well and checked their background so as to avoid hiring "drama magnets," as she liked to call them—those women who just seem to draw drama wherever they go. Sheila vowed that there would be no such employees causing any kind of nonsense in her place of business.

She was much too classy for that. Tony always said his wife was full of elegance, grace, and wisdom, and that he knew he'd married the woman of Proverbs 31, the virtuous woman described in the Bible, the woman who has herself together in every way and is a complement to her man.

It was a little after 10:00 in the morning when Kim finished cleaning the kitchen at the Boston house and was about to head to the spa. Tony told her he was planning to go to the spa and get a massage from his wife. He wanted it to be a surprise visit, so he asked Kim not to say anything. Tony had only been to the spa on one other occasion, and that was the grand opening. He'd been promising Sheila he'd soon come back for the royal treatment and thought today would be perfect so he could look extra fresh at the ball tonight.

Sheila was a masseuse and he always told her that her hands were incredible. They worked magic on his body.

Trey came in the kitchen. "Hey Dad, I thought you were about to head to the barbershop."

"Yeah I am, then after that I'm going to your mom's spa for a facial, manicure, and massage. You know, I'm gonna be in the spotlight tonight so I wanna look good."

"I hear you, Dad. I was just talking to Todd about doing the same thing. So we're gonna go get our hair cut now and then we'll probably see you at the spa. Come on Todd, let's go, man," Trey yelled upstairs.

Kim arrived at the spa and walked over to Sheila when she saw her working on a client. "Hi Miss Sheila, I'm here."

"Hey Kim, thanks so much for coming in. As you can see, we really need you. You can handle the reception area for now because that phone has been ringing off the hook."

"Okay, sure," Kim said, and headed for the reception area.

"Hey Kim, did you see I added some more Barack Obama campaign signs in front of the spa?" Sheila asked.

"I sure did, Miss Sheila, and I'm so glad to see them out there." Kim smiled.

It was the 2008 election year, and everyone was so excited that for the first time it appeared there would an African-American president. Barack Obama had just become the Democratic nominee, and African Americans all over were especially proud of the smart, young black senator from Illinois. The Boston family loved Obama, just like most of the nation—and the world for that matter. Tony, Sheila, Trey, and even Todd had sent separate donations to his campaign, and Todd had volunteered for the Obama campaign in Atlanta. Tony put Obama campaign signs in front of the law firm and at the house. They were all trying to do their part to make sure Obama would be elected president.

Just before noon, Tony walked into the spa. Sheila had her back turned, so he quietly tiptoed over, slipped his arms around her waist, and kissed her on the neck.

"Ooh," she said, "whoever this is kissing me better be one of two people, either my husband Tony or Barack Obama, because aside from my husband, that's the only other man I could be interested in." She turned around laughing. Tony kissed her on the cheek.

"Wait a minute. What do you mean, Barack Obama is the only other man you could be interested in? You'd better not be interested in any other man besides me. Plus, how dare you put me up against a guy like Barack? I mean, I know I'm smart and handsome, but I'm no match for Barack. That man is a genius, plus he's smooth, classy, and got all the ladies falling for him. Barack is in a class all by himself. So you can't compare me to a man like that, that's just not fair." Tony smiled and looked around at all the ladies in the spa, expecting them to agree with him. Sheila laughed and kissed him on the cheek.

"Oh no, don't try to make up now. I want the truth, would you really leave me for Barack?" Tony smiled.

"In a heartbeat, baby, and I'm just keeping it real," Sheila said, as every woman within the sound of her voice laughed. Sheila hugged Tony. "I wouldn't leave you, baby."

"Oh no, that's okay." Tony said, pulling away from her. "Because you see, if you leave me for Barack that just frees me up to head on out to Chicago and get me a new woman—you know, a nice, intelligent, classy, powerful, sexy black woman

like Michelle Obama or Oprah. So you go on and get Barack."
Tony had everybody in the place falling out laughing.

Sheila put her hand on Tony's shoulder. "Okay baby, you win.
Besides, Michelle and Oprah got it going on way too much for
me to try to compete against either of them, so I guess it looks
like you and I are stuck with each other for now. And actually,
that's a good thing, because I love you, Mr. Boston," she said,
hugging her husband.

"I love you too, Mrs. Boston." Tony kissed her on the forehead.

Kim walked over. "So what brings you here today, Mr. Tony?"
She tried to pretend like she wasn't aware he was coming.

"Well, I was hoping my wife would give me the royal treatment today—you know, the kind that includes the spa ser-
vices. She can give me the husbandly royal treatment later at
home." He raised his eyebrows at Sheila.

"You are too funny, Mr. Tony," Kim said, laughing. "Miss Sheila, do you want me to take him to your area?" Kim asked.

"Uh, actually, take him over to Deborah. I'm going to let her
give him a manicure and pedicure first," Sheila said, looking
at Tony's hands.

"Okay, come on Mr. Tony." Kim pulled him by the arm. She
introduced Tony to Deborah, one of the nail technicians.

♥ Chapter 21 ♥

The time had finally arrived for the highly anticipated Boston & Associates Annual Charity Ball. It was a huge event and everybody that was anybody in the Maryland area usually attended, including elected officials and local celebrities. All of the Bostons were excited. Kendra was so happy to be a part of it, she decided she was going to forget all about her father and the rape incident and all that pain and really enjoy herself tonight. This was the first time she would be going to such a lavish event and she wanted it to be special. Not to mention the fact that she was going to be in the company of a man whom she was falling in love with.

The event was being held at the beautiful Hyatt Regency Hotel at the Inner Harbor.

Tony and Sheila walked in looking stunning. Trey and Kendra walk in behind them, arm in arm, looking just as amazing. Then Todd and Brittney walked in arm in arm, as fly as they could be. All the men were dressed in black tuxedos. Sheila and Kendra both wore beautiful black gowns. Kim wore a red gown and was escorted by a guy named Mario, who was doing his residency at the same hospital where she was doing

her clinical trials. Sean and Joe showed up walking hand in
hand with their dates. They sat at Trey and Todd's table. The
evening was spectacular, with wonderful performances, good
food, live auctions, and lots of mingling.

"So Todd, have you met anybody famous since you been in
the ATL?" Joe asked.

"No, not yet, I'm sure I will soon."

"Well, you're in the right place, because a lot of celebrities
live in Atlanta," Joe said.

Tony eventually stepped to the microphone and thanked
everyone for coming out. He also spoke about how important
the evening was and how the money raised would go to a very
good cause.

As the evening continued, Kendra and Trey spent a lot of
time on the dance floor, and everybody jumped up when the
electric slide came on.

At the end of the night, the DJ played mostly slow songs.
Trey and Kendra danced, looking into each other's eyes. They
were falling for each other.

"I know I've already told you this, but you look absolutely
beautiful tonight, Miss Jackson," Trey whispered in her ear as
he danced close to her.

"Thank you, Mr. Boston. You're looking incredibly handsome
yourself," Kendra said.

"I have a surprise for you tonight, baby," Trey said, looking
deep into her eyes.

"Oh, what's that?" she asked.

"I reserved a room for us in this hotel tonight so we wouldn't
have to drive all the way home." Trey smiled.

"Oh yeah, and who says I trust you enough to stay in a hotel
room with you all night, Mr. Boston?" Kendra smiled back,
trying to play off the fact that she didn't really like the idea.

"I already paid for the room. You're not going to make me
waste my money, are you?" Trey said, with a pitiful look on his

face.

"I don't want you to think anything's going to happen, because I'm not ready for that yet, Trey. I already told you, I am determined to wait until after marriage to have sex. I don't want to commit fornication."

"Nothing will happen, Kendra. You just seem very stressed lately, and I want you to have a beautiful night. We've spent the night together before and nothing happened, so tonight will be no different. I want you to have a great time, and I want you to trust me. I won't force you into anything, I promise." Trey kissed her on the forehead.

As the crowd started to disperse, Trey and Kendra said goodbye to Tony, Sheila, and the rest of the family and made their way upstairs to the hotel room.

Trey slipped the credit card style key into the door and pushed it open when he heard the lock click. He and Kendra stepped inside. She was astonished at how beautiful the room was. Trey had pre-ordered some champagne, which was on ice in the romantic sitting area of the room. He then pulled a small overnight bag from underneath the bed.

"What's in there?" Kendra asked.

"Just a few things we'll need for the night," he said as he sucked his teeth and gave her a sexy glance. "No, let me stop, I'm just messing with you," he said, laughing.

"Oh, so you had this thing all planned out, huh? When did you bring the bag in here? And is there anything in there for me?"

"Oh yeah, it's something in here for you, sure is. And I brought it in here a little earlier, when I left the table and told you I had to go use the restroom. I actually went to the car, grabbed the bag, then got the keys from the front desk and managed to get back to the ball before you suspected anything."

"You are something else, Mr. Boston."

"And so are you, Miss Jackson."

Trey pulled out a Keith Sweat CD and played his favorite

romantic, old-school song, "Make It Last Forever." When Kendra heard the song she went crazy.

"Oh my goodness, I love this song! Oooooh and I love Keith Sweat. I used to just sit and listen to this CD over and over and over again and wish I was in love. Just hearing his music made me wanna be madly in love with somebody. Plus I used to have the biggest crush on Keith Sweat." Kendra had a dreamy-eyed look as she took the champagne glass Trey handed her and sat down on the leather love seat in the sitting area.

Trey was so happy that she was excited. He hoped the beautiful room and the relaxing setting would help her to unwind. She had been preoccupied lately, worried about something, but he didn't know what. He figured she was sad because her mother's birthday had recently passed and that maybe she was thinking about her.

They took a couple of sips of champagne and Trey asked for a dance.

"We've been dancing all night. You want to dance again?" she asked.

"This dance is different. We're all alone up here in our own private room and I selected the music that I want to hear," he said, as he extended his hand to her. Kendra put her hand in his and he slowly pulled her close to him in slow dance position.

First their eyes met as they grooved to the music and seemed to lose themselves in the moment. Then their lips met as they as they began to kiss. Trey slowly slid his hand along Kendra's face and neck and gently pulled the hairpin from her hair, as it fell around her face. He put both his hands in her hair and continued kissing her. Kendra started to get nervous, because she didn't want to go too far and pulled away.

"Hey, look at me," Trey said. "I just want you to relax, baby. I'm not going to try to make love to you. I just want you to have a night to be free, because I can see in your eyes that you need that. I want you to trust me Kendra, because I, I, uh, I love you, baby."

"Oh Trey, you are so wonderful. I love you too." Tears filled her eyes and they shared another kiss.

Trey spent the rest of the night pampering Kendra and treating her like a queen. He'd asked his mother for some massage oils from the spa and gave Kendra a wonderful hot-oil massage. They spent rest of the night talking, until Kendra fell asleep in his arms.

♥ <u>Chapter 22</u> ♥

*M*orning came and Trey was still tired when he woke up. He looked over at Kendra as she slept peacefully. Trey smiled as thoughts of their night together passed through his mind. He thought about how special Kendra was to him and felt like their night together took their relationship to a whole new level, especially since they'd confessed their love for one another. Trey gently brushed Kendra's face and thought about how much he wanted to settle down and get married and that she could be the one. He believed Kendra was really into him, but sometimes he felt like she was holding back her heart on purpose, almost as if she was afraid to let him completely in. He figured that she must still have a lot of pain inside from losing her mother, which was probably why she sometimes looked sad.

Trey got up and ordered breakfast. The sound of him running water woke Kendra out of her sleep. As she laid there in bed, she looked around, once again noticing how lovely the room was. *A beautiful room for a beautiful night,* she thought. She continued to lie there staring at the ceiling, feeling both happy and sad. Happy because she and Trey had an incredible night and she now knew he loved her, and sad because she felt like she was doing wrong by him because of the way she set out to meet him, and the fact that she still hadn't been honest about who her father was. Kendra prayed that Trey would forgive her and still want to be with her when he found out. She also wanted them to talk about how they were going to move forward in the relationship. Because she wanted to wait for marriage to have sex, she thought that might push Trey away. *Boy, is anything ever easy in life?* she thought.

Trey came out of the bathroom and saw that she was awake. "Good morning beautiful," he said as he walked over and kissed her on the forehead.

"Good morning, Trey."

"How did you sleep, baby?"

"I slept very, very, very well," she said, smiling, "and how did you sleep, Mr. Boston?"

"I slept pretty good too, but I still feel a little tired."

"Thanks, Trey, for a wonderful evening and a fantastic night. You are an incredible man and I thank God that you are in my life." Tears filled her eyes.

"Ah baby, you are so sweet. I thank God for you too. You are a beautiful woman inside and out. The kind of woman I really want in my life, Kendra." He kissed her once more on her forehead.

"Room service," the male voice on the other side of the door yelled as they heard a knock on the door. Trey walked over to let him in as Kendra quickly scooted off to the bathroom. When she returned Trey was waiting at the table with the food.

"Come join me for breakfast, sweetie," he said.

Kendra felt as if she were in a fairytale. This was the life she'd always dreamed about, but before she met Trey it seemed so inconceivable, especially because of her painful past and the depression she experienced for years.

She joined Trey at the table and sat gazing into his eyes. There was so much she wanted to tell him and so much she wanted to experience with him, but for now she wanted to just enjoy the moment.

♥ Chapter 23 ♥

*I*t didn't seem like your typical Sunday at the Boston house. Everyone slept well past one o'clock, and even though Todd was back in his old room, there was no smell of fresh biscuits to wake him up. They all needed to rest after a late night.

It was about 1:45 in the afternoon when Trey walked in. As he walked upstairs to Todd's room, he heard some laughter in the basement. He assumed it was probably Todd talking on the phone and decided to go down and have a few words with him. He also wanted to confirm the time of his flight because he was the one taking him to the airport. When Trey was half-way down the stairs, he could hear two voices instead of one. It sounded like Todd had brought Brittney back to the house and Trey was hoping that she hadn't spent the night, because Mom and Pops didn't play that.

"Who's that?" Todd asked, when he heard footsteps.

"It's Trey, can I come down?"

"Yeah, come on down, man."

"Hello," Trey said when he saw Brittney sitting on one of the barstools.

"Hi Trey," she answered, smiling.

"Whassup, man?" Todd said.

Trey realized the young lady must not have slept there because she had on a sweat suit instead of her gown from last night. Plus he knew Todd had more sense than that.

"Hey man, whassup with you?" Trey asked.

"I'm just chillin', about to check out this game. It's gonna be nice watching the Ravens play for a change. That's one thing about being in Atlanta, I miss watching Ray Lewis and the boys play on Sundays." Todd flipped through the channels with the remote.

"You'll just have to become a Falcons fan for the next four years," Trey replied.

"Yeah, the Falcons are cool too.

"So what time is your flight?"

"Not until seven forty-five."

"Alright, I'm gonna go next door and chill for a while and I'll be ready to take y'all to the airport at about six. Cool?" Trey asked as he headed toward the stairs.

"Yeah, that's cool, man, thanks."

Kendra felt as if she were walking on air. She kept looking at all the pictures they'd taken at the ball the night before and marveled at how good she and Trey looked together. There was no denying, she was in love with this man.

As she felt love fill on one side of her heart, the other side felt like it was filled with pain, and after twelve years she was starting to feel like she'd had enough. "I want to be happy," she said in a low voice, as she zeroed in on Trey in the pictures. "Somehow I have got to tell you about my father and pray that you forgive me."

She knew her first step was to stand up to her father, and tell him that she was in love with Trey and that she was not going to do anything to hurt him or Tony. She also wanted to tell her father that she thought he really had raped that girl and that she wanted him to pray and ask for forgiveness and change his ways.

Even though it was Sunday, Kendra was in no mood for the doom and gloom of going to see her father. She was on a serious high and wanted it to last for as long as it could. She had no intentions of abandoning her father because she still loved him dearly; however, she was going to put an end to his request for her to take down the Boston family. She didn't want to think about the confrontation they were sure to have.

Kim walked in the front door as Trey came upstairs from the basement.

"Hey Kim," Trey said, walking over to help her.

"Hi Trey, how are you?"

"What are you doing here? I thought you said my Mom gave you the day off."

"She did. I just stopped by to pick up some of my things I left over here. I need them because I'm going out on a date tonight." She smiled.

"Cool. Is it with the same guy from last night?" Trey asked, smiling back at her.

"Yep, sure is."

"Oh…so do you like him?"

"He seems nice so far. I would like to get to know him better."

"So what are y'all doing tonight?"

"We're going to see a movie and get a little bite to eat."

"Well, it's nice to see you going out, Kim. Like I told you before, you deserve to have somebody in your life who will treat you right."

"Goodness Trey, slow down. This is only the second date. I wouldn't say that he's in my life." She shook her head. "Wait a minute, you're not jealous because another guy is taking me out, are you?" She smirked.

"Don't be silly, girl, why would I be jealous? I'm already seeing someone that I'm in—" Trey caught himself before he said the "L" word in front of Kim. He didn't want to hurt her feelings so he softened it up a bit. "I'm in a relationship with someone I care for, and besides, if I really wanted you, Kim, I could have you." He grinned as he walked toward the front door. "And to answer your question, I'm not jealous, I'm just happy for you, baby girl. Make sure you tell him I said he'd better treat you like the queen you are, or he'll have to answer to me."

"You're so full of yourself, Trey. And by the way, I could have you too, if I really wanted you." Kim smiled and walked into the kitchen.

♥ Chapter 24 ♥

*I*t was midweek and Kendra pulled into her apartment complex after a long day at work. She stopped at her mailbox before heading in and noticed a letter from her father. Kendra walked into her apartment and sat down on the couch. She went through all of her other mail before opening her father's letter, which felt rather thick.

As she began reading the letter, tears streamed down her face. Her father accused her of forgetting about him sitting there in prison. He told her he couldn't believe she'd missed two Sunday visits in a matter of weeks. He asked her to please come and see him because he felt his life was hopeless without her. He also expressed concern about Kendra possibly developing feelings for Trey and forgetting about their original plan.

After reading the letter, Kendra knew she had to stand up to her father in order to put an end to the confusion and pain that she felt. She made up her mind that she was going to come clean with him about everything, including her feelings for Trey, her meeting with Rhonda, and the fact that she believes he was unfaithful in his marriage to her mother. Kendra also wanted to let her father know that she loved him, but was disappointed in the way he had lived his life. She decided it was time to tell him that if he didn't change and try to live right, she was going to limit her association with him.

Kendra fell to her knees in prayer. She knew she needed God's guidance for this.

The next day Trey called Kendra and asked her to help him with his house hunting.

"I've been thinking about moving for quite some time," he told her. "I never intended to stay in my parents' in-law suite this long. I only moved back to save some money while I was going to law school. I told you I used to live in my own townhouse out in Columbia a couple of years back. Now I'm ready to buy a house and that's one of the places where I'd like to live again. So can you go with me?" he asked.

"Sure, I'll go with you," she said, happy that he wanted her opinion on his new house. "I have great taste with that sort of thing so, sure, I'll be glad to help you. Just one stipulation: You can't move too far away from me." Kendra giggled.

"Oh, you don't have to worry about that. Plus I think God has some special plans for us, so I need to stay close to you anyway," Trey said in his usual sincere manner.

Kendra met Trey at his house after work. It was the first time he'd seen her since they said I love you to one another.

"Hey there handsome, how are you?"

"I'm great now that you're here. Come on, get in my car. I'll drive because you look tired," Trey said as he helped her out of the car. "My agent is going to show us four houses."

"Okay, is your agent meeting us here?"

"No, she's meeting us at the properties."

It took about two hours to see all the houses. Both Trey and Kendra fell in love with one in particular. It was a huge, brick, single-family home with six bedrooms, hardwood floors, nine-foot ceilings, three fireplaces, finished basement, gorgeous deck, and a nice wood-fenced backyard. The house was located in Columbia, the area he preferred. Trey told the real estate agent that he wanted to see a few more properties before making a decision.

"Is your girlfriend going to be moving in with you?" the agent asked.

"Uh, that's not the plan right now but her opinion is very important to me, and who knows what the future may hold." Trey put his arm around Kendra.

They said goodbye to the agent and drove back to get Kendra's car.

"Trey, when are you going to teach me how to drive a stick? you keep promising me but never get around to it."

"Oh my bad, we'll do that next week some time for sure.

When they arrived at Trey's house, Kendra got back into her car, they kissed, and she drove off.

♥ <u>Chapter 25</u> ♥

"Can I help you?" the receptionist at the Paradise Day Spa asked.

"Yes, my name is Kendra Jackson. I have an appointment with Sheila Boston for the royal treatment."

"Okay, Ms. Jackson, we have you down for nine o'clock. You can sign in and have a seat. Someone will be right with you."

"Thank you."

Kendra took a seat in the waiting area. It was her first time there and she noticed how beautiful and classy the place was. She felt both excited and nervous about her visit with Miss Sheila, because she knew she was hiding so much and Miss Sheila seemed to be such a discerning woman.

Kendra felt a connection to Miss Sheila and knew she was someone she could look up to like a mother figure.

"Hello, pretty one," Sheila said when she saw Kendra in the waiting area.

"Hi, Miss Sheila," Kendra said, as she got up to give her a hug.

"It's nice to see you, Kendra. Come on back."

"It's nice to see you too, Miss Sheila. I tell you, I am long overdue for a manicure, pedicure, facial, and definitely a massage, because I am so stressed out."

"Well, you've come to the right place, honey, but why are you stressed out? You're too young and too pretty to be stressed."

"Well, for one, law school is no joke. And Trey and I have been seeing quite a bit of each other, plus I'm trying to keep up with my full-time job, and I guess it's just a little stressful trying to balance everything."

"Well, sweetie, you're just going to have to let Trey know that you can't see as much of him during the week when you have class, and is there any way you can cut down your hours at work or maybe work part-time?"

"Not right now because I really need the money. And I don't want to cut back on seeing Trey because he and I have become so close and well, I'm...I'm in love with him," Kendra said. She flashed a smile that seemed to light the entire room.

"Wow! Okay. Um...I don't know exactly what to say to that!" Sheila said, raising her eyebrows.

"What? Do you think I'm moving too fast? Or what, you don't think he feels the same way about me?" Kendra asked with a look of concern.

"Well honey, I'll tell you like this: No one but Trey can answer how he feels about you, and only you can answer the question of whether you feel you're moving too fast. You know, God has a way of speaking to us and letting us feel His message through our gut instinct. You know how sometimes you feel confused or unsure about how to handle a situation or you wonder whether you're doing the right thing? Well, if you pray about it and then you start to feel comfortable with it and at ease with your decision, that's God giving you peace with it, which usually means He's blessing your decision. Then there are those times when you struggle and ponder over a decision and just don't seem satisfied or at ease with a choice you've made, like you're not at peace or your gut feeling says *wait, this isn't right.* That's when you know you should slow down, keep praying and seeking God's guidance, and let Him guide you through what's best for you." Sheila said.

Kendra paid close attention, like she was clinging to her every word. Sheila could sense that Kendra needed to talk, so she continued. "Now as far as Trey is concerned, Kendra, he's a great young man and I am very proud of my son, but no matter how good a guy you think you're with, you can't rush love and you can't force it. Love is something that has to happen naturally, and when you feel love for someone and that love is reciprocated, it can be a beautiful thing. But when it's rushed or when it's unsure, it can be painful. Now, you're a smart, young woman, Kendra, and when you feel within your heart that you are in love with a man to the point where you don't have to question whether he feels the same about you, then you know that's real love, and it's worth taking your time to get to that point. Also, when you feel relaxed with where God has you in your relationship with Trey or any other man whom you wish to be with, then you won't have to question whether or not you're moving too fast, because you'll know within your heart that you are exactly where God wants you to be, as long as you always pray and put God first." As Sheila finished her last sentence, she could see tears filling up in Kendra's eyes, so she reached over and hugged her.

Kendra hugged Miss Sheila back, squeezing her tightly. *God, it feels so good to have an older woman talk to her,* she thought. She really missed being able to talk to her own mother.

"Thank you so much, Miss Sheila. I really needed that," Kendra said, as she wiped her eyes.

"No problem, sweetie. Now come on, let's get you that royal treatment."

♥ <u>Chapter 26</u> ♥

*T*rey and Kendra returned to her apartment about 10:30 after a night out with his buddies and their dates at a bull roast. Kendra sat beside Trey on the sofa. "Your friend Sean is crazy. I can't believe he had everybody doing the electric slide to that slow song," she said, laughing.

"Yeah, that fool is crazy. That's my boy though. Huh, if you think he's crazy now, you should have seen that fool back in high school. He kept me and Joe in trouble," Trey said, laughing with her. "The three of us have been boys ever since elementary school, and then we all went to college together."

"Yeah, I could tell by the way they were talking about all the girls you had back in the day." Kendra smirked at Trey.

"Ah, come on now, you can't believe everything those fools say. Half the time, they're just talking stuff just to make people laugh, that's all."

"Oh, so the part about how all the girls were always trying to get with you, and the part about they had to lie for you constantly in college when you were with one girl and another girl was looking for you, was all a lie?

"Hold up, baby, those were my crazy college days so why

are we talking about this?" He slid close to her. "I'd much rather talk about you and me." He started kissing her on the neck. "Right now you're the only woman on my mind."

"Am I really? How do I know that?"

Her words stopped Trey cold. He looked at Kendra with surprise. "What is that supposed to mean?" he asked.

"How do I know that I'm the only woman on your mind?"

"Do you mean besides the fact that I just told you so, Kendra? How about the fact that I spend the majority of my free time with you? How about the fact that I spend more time with you than I have ever spent with any other woman? How about the fact that I treat you like a queen and show you lots of attention and affection and we're not even sleeping together, but I'm still around?" Trey said, obviously irritated.

Kendra looked at him, speechless. "What? Is that all you want me for, sex?" She raised her voice slightly.

"Oh my goodness, that is not what I said and you know it. Okay, you know what, we're not in court so I don't feel like arguing a case tonight, nor do I feel like any drama, so can we please just have a nice quiet night together?" Trey grabbed her hand.

"Come here, sit on my lap," he said, pulling her over by her arm. She had a hard time sitting all the way down on his lap because her jeans were a little tight. Trey started laughing, then he noticed that she had tears in her eyes. "Baby, what's the matter?" he asked as he put her face in his chest.

"Nothing, I'm fine," she answered.

"Why are you crying, Kendra?"

"I don't know. I guess I just want to make sure that you're serious about me, and I'm stressed out over school and everything else that I'm dealing with."

"Come here, baby." Trey slid her off his lap and got on his knees in front of her. "Kendra, I am very serious about you. I'm crazy about you, woman. Sometimes men don't always say or do the right things at the right times and maybe I should have told you this before, but you are definitely the only woman that I am seeing and the only woman that I want to see. I love you, baby, and I want us to be together. To tell you the truth, sometimes I feel like you're holding back on me, not just sexually, but like you're afraid to let me all the way into your heart. It sometimes feels like you want me around but that you're either afraid or insecure about something, and I just can't put my finger on it." Trey lifted her chin so he could look into her eyes. "Stop worrying so much, and please don't be so insecure."

"Oh Trey, I really love you too, but everything is so complicated." She covered her face with her hands.

"What are you talking about 'complicated,' Kendra? Is there somebody else in your life? Do you have a man somewhere I don't know about?"

"No, you're the only man I'm seeing, and the only man I want to see. It's just that—"

Trey's phone rang before she could finish her sentence. He looked down and saw that it was his mother calling. "Wait a minute, baby, I need to get this. It's my mom and she doesn't usually call me this late from her cell phone." He answered the phone. "Hello Ma, are you okay?"

"Hi Trey, are you driving right now?" Sheila asked, sounding upset.

"No, I'm not. Ma, what's the matter?"

"It's your grandmother. She just passed away at the hospital."

"What, are you serious, Grandma died? What happened to her? I just talked to her the other day and told her about the house I was looking at. She sounded fine." He shook his head.

"They're not sure. They think it may have been a stroke. Your Aunt Brenda found her on the bathroom floor and she wasn't breathing. By the time they got her to the hospital, she had already passed."

"Ma, I'm so sorry. Are you okay?"

"Yeah, I'm okay, baby. Your father's here with me at the hospital. I'm not going to tell Todd until the morning, so don't call him. I don't want to upset him this late."

"Okay, Ma. I love you."

"I love you too. Be careful."

Trey hung up the phone and hung his head.

"I'm sorry about your grandmother, Trey." Kendra wrapped her arms around him.

They both began to cry, each for their own reasons. Both of them felt their own pain, yet both were silent.

After a few minutes Kendra broke the silence. "So your mom is the youngest of all her sisters?

"Yeah, she's the baby of the family."

"You said your Grandmother used to be a nurse. Which hospital did she work at?" Kendra asked, wanting Trey to talk about his grandmother, hoping it would help cheer him up a little. It seemed to make a difference because after a while he was laughing, talking about how he and his cousins used to go over her house when they were younger and race on their bikes and have a good time.

Trey got up to use the bathroom. When he came out, Kendra was in the kitchen pouring iced tea into two glasses. "Come here, baby," he said as he stood in the hallway. Trey took Kendra by the hand and led her into the bedroom. He started kissing her.

"I love you, baby."

"I love you too, Trey."

He continued kissing her, and started gently caressing her arms. He then sat down on the bed as he pulled her in front of him. Kendra looked into Trey's eyes and could see his vulnerability. "I need you tonight, baby," he said as he laid her down on the bed. In his mind he was begging her not to stop him, not tonight. Kendra was feeling a little weak as well. All the emotional drama had left her feeling just as vulnerable. Trey's kisses became more passionate and Kendra could feel things really heating up. She then whispered in his ear, "I'm not ready, Trey. I can't do this. I don't want to disappoint God. I'm saving myself for marriage."

Trey rolled off her and his head hit the pillow. They laid there in silence, staring at the ceiling.

"Kendra, I'm sorry. I can certainly understand that you want to live right and I really like that. Believe it or not, I want to live right too and I would like to wait until after marriage to have sex, but sometimes it's just so hard. I mean I love you and I want to make love to you so bad. But, the closer I get to God, the more I realize how much I don't want to sin, so we're going to have to keep praying and you're going to have to keep stopping things before they go all the way with us, because it's obvious you're the stronger one. Oh, and it might help if you stop wearing them sexy jeans, I mean, a brother can only take so much."

"You got it, baby, she said smiling. Thanks for understanding and for wanting to do the right thing, Trey." Kendra curled up next to him and fell asleep in his arms.

♥ *Chapter 27* ♥

The Boston family spent the next few days making funeral arrangements and helping Sheila and her sisters with whatever they needed. Kim was a huge help and did a fantastic job cooking, cleaning, and keeping everything and everyone together. Todd came home for a couple of days and he and Trey found some time to work together on Trey's car.

The family was surprised at how well Sheila and her sisters held up at their mom's funeral, especially since her death was so sudden. She seemed so healthy and really took care of herself, so her death was such a shock. Todd and Trey took it hard, because they were really close to their grandmother.

As it was getting late, most of the family members started headed back home, especially the ones from out of town.

Kendra told Trey she was going to head home to give him time to spend with his family. He told her he would call her later.

On the way home, Kendra felt really sad. She hated funerals because they brought back so many memories of when she buried her mom. Going to that funeral had her thinking a lot about both her mom and her dad. She decided she would go home and write her dad a letter. After all, she felt bad that she hadn't been to see him in a couple of weeks. She wanted to write to him and explain how law school and work were keeping her busy but that she was coming to see him on Sunday.

When Sunday arrived, Kendra went to early service at church and prayed about the entire situation with her father. She really felt like God had given her the strength to finally stand up to her father in a respectable way and tell him how she felt.

When Kendra arrived at the prison, she sat down in the visiting room and saw her father's cellmate, Mr. Wayne. She waved to him and he walked over to speak to her.

"Hello Mr. Wayne, how are you?" Kendra asked.

"I'm okay, can't wait to get out of here. How are you doing, Kendra?" Wayne asked.

"I'm fine."

"That's good."

"Well, I finally get out of here for good in exactly two weeks and one day, and I can't wait. It's been nearly thirteen long years and I can't take it anymore. I must say I'm a changed man, God knows I am." He shook his head. "God used this time to speak to my heart and change me and from now on I am going to do right." He smiled.

"Well, God bless you, Mr. Wayne. I am so happy for you. You just keep praying and walking in faith and God will work it all out for you." Kendra smiled back at him.

When Rob walked through the door, he smiled happily when he saw Kendra, but his look quickly changed to one of anger when he saw Wayne standing in front of her having a conversation. Rob was protective of his daughter, and the thought of another man being close to her or touching her made him sick, probably because deep down inside he knew how he used to prey on young girls and take advantage of them. It was ironic that he felt this way, because he actually wanted his daughter to purposely get close to a man so she could destroy that man's father.

"Well, look who decided to show up," Rob said, rudely interrupting Kendra and Wayne's conversation. "Hello, baby girl," he said, hugging Kendra.

"Hello, Daddy," she said, smiling.

Wayne turned to Kendra. "It was good seeing you again. You two have a great visit," he said as he walked away.

"Have a seat baby girl," Rob said, smiling. "It's really good to see you. I missed you so much, Kendra. You know you're my inspiration. You're what keeps me going in here and the reason I want to get out of here. So tell me, what's been keeping you away from me?" He looked concerned.

"It's just been a lot going on, Daddy. I started law school and it's really tough, plus I'm still working full time and I've been going to church a lot and singing on the choir, and uh..." She hesitated before continuing. "Uh, I'm just trying to get my life together," she said, looking at him with a half smile.

"So does getting your life together mean forgetting about your father in prison?"

"No. It doesn't mean that at all. It just means that I'm only one person and I'm doing the best that I can."

"So where does that Boston boy, Trey, fit into all this—or should I say, how is our plan going? That is, if it still is a plan." He smirked.

"Actually, Daddy, it's not a plan anymore. I've made up my mind that I don't want to have any part of that," she said, looking him straight in the eye with no sign of fear.

"Well, well, well, what do we have here? I guess Tony Boston taught his son some of his slick tactics. Is that why you're changing up on your own father, huh?" A look of anger passed across his face, but Kendra stood her ground.

"Dad, it has nothing to do with Trey using any slick tactics on me. I don't see the point of doing anything to harm that family, first of all. Plus, that was your plan, not mine. I am not that kind of person. I happen to like Trey very much. He is a wonderful man. Daddy, I've been going to church on a regular basis like I used to with Mom, and I've been praying that God would take my pain away and make me whole and happy, and I am praying for you too." Tears filled her eyes.

"Oh yeah, what are you praying for me for? I'm in jail."

"I'm praying that God will give you a spirit of forgiveness and truth. I'm praying that you will come clean with me and tell me the truth about what really happened."

"What are you talking about, tell you the truth? Did Tony Boston get through to you and turn you against me too, like he did with my jury? I have told you the truth. I was innocent and my lawyer stopped defending me during my trial. That's the truth," he said angrily.

"Is it? Daddy, I deserve the whole truth. My mother is dead and my father is in jail. I have nothing, at least let me have the truth. And you know what else, going to church has helped me to forgive you, Daddy, but I want the truth. Did you really rape that girl? And did you cheat on my mother?" Tears streamed down Kendra's face.

Rob looked at the floor, shaking his head, as the anger slowly disappeared from his face. He held his head down for a while, unable to look at Kendra. When he looked up, he had tears in his eyes.

"You've obviously made your choice, baby girl. I don't know if it's the Lord that you've chosen over me or if it's that Boston boy, but whatever it is, I hope it makes you happy because I'm very disappointed in you." A tear rolled down his face, and he got up to walk away.

"Daddy, wait," Kendra said, standing to her feet. Rob stopped and looked back at her. "Daddy, please, let's talk about this."

Rob shook his head, then turned and walked away.

Kendra stood watching as he walked out of the room. She dropped her head and left the prison, completely devastated, like she'd just lost her best friend.

Wayne was sitting close by and once again heard their conversation. He hated the way Rob manipulated his daughter. He wished Kendra could see the truth about her father—that he was nothing but a con artist and a user, and from some of the stories he'd told Wayne, he'd been using people for most of his adult life. Wayne had tried for years to change Rob's mind about trying to get even with Tony Boston and was upset when he found out Rob wanted to use his own daughter to help him do it. *What a lowdown pig he is,* Wayne thought. Someone had to put a stop to Rob, and with only two weeks left, if he was going to do it, he had to act quickly.

♥ Chapter 28 ♥

Monday night, Trey and the boys were having a good time at the game. Trey was a bit worried because he hadn't spoken to Kendra since Sunday morning and that wasn't like her. He'd tried to call her several times but didn't get an answer.

During halftime, he tried her number again. This time she answered. "Kendra, hey baby, are you okay?" Trey asked. He put his hand over his ear to block the noise of the crowd.

"Yes, Trey, I'm fine. I'm just not feeling well."

"I'm sorry you're not feeling well, baby. Do you need anything?"

"No, just some rest and I'll be fine." She sounded like she was completely out of it.

"Have you been sleeping all this time? I've been trying to reach you since yesterday." He was very concerned.

"Yeah, I've been sleeping. I took some medicine that makes me drowsy and it's still having an affect on me, so I'm going to get some more sleep and I'll call you later."

"Okay baby, hope you feel well soon."

"Thanks, Trey."

When Trey hung up the phone, he was concerned. She really didn't sound well. He decided he was going to go over and check on her first thing in the morning.

Trey tried to enjoy the game with his boys. He, Sean, and Joe had gotten tickets to see the Washington Wizards play the L.A. Lakers at the Verizon Center in D.C. The score was tied and going into overtime and the crowd was hyped. A lot of the people in the crowd were cheering for the Lakers, but not Sean. He was a true fan of Antwan Jamison of the Wizards.

"That's right Antwan take it to the hoop, take it to the hoop," Sean hollered when he saw him about to score. "Damn, that boy's bad, y'all! See, that's how I ball. That's how I handle y'all on the court." He gave Trey and Joe a high five. "Everybody's always talking about how they wanna be like Mike, they need to be talking about how they wanna be like Sean, because I'm the man."

"Man, shut up and watch the game. You're always running your mouth," Joe said as he and Trey started laughing.

When Kendra hung up the phone after talking to Trey, she almost called him back and asked him to come over, but she couldn't bring herself to do it. She was hurt and depressed over yesterday's visit with her father and wanted somebody to talk to. She got out of bed and walked to the bathroom. As she washed her face, tears started streaming from her eyes. Kendra felt so trapped and confused. She wanted to do the right thing but didn't want to lose her father while doing it.

She realized that really doing the right thing meant she must come clean with Trey. How could she demand and expect her father to come clean with her if she couldn't do the same? She decided she was going to have a long talk with Trey tomorrow evening. She prayed that he would understand and forgive her and want to continue seeing her. She knew she'd be devastated if he decided to break things off. *Oh no,* she thought.

What if I lose both my father and Trey? She decided she was going to pray and walk in faith.

♥ <u>Chapter 29</u> ♥

Kendra called Trey the next morning to tell him that she was feeling better. She asked if he could come by after work. Trey agreed.

Kendra spent the afternoon trying to focus on her schoolwork as best as she could. She kept looking at the clock to see how much longer it would be before she would have her talk with Trey.

She finished her schoolwork at about three o'clock and watched TV for a while. She knew Trey would be there about six and would probably be hungry, so she put some dinner on. She took a shower and put on a sweat suit so she could be comfortable. Kendra felt very nervous about the conversation she was about to have with Trey.

A little after six, Trey knocked on the door. Kendra's heart pounded, and she paused for a moment to compose herself before opening the door.

"Hey baby, how are you feeling?" Trey asked as he reached to hug her.

"I'm feeling better, Trey, thanks for coming over. Are you hungry?"

"I'm starving. I rushed through my work so I could get here as soon as possible and didn't get a chance to eat lunch. Umm, something smells good. Did you cook?"

"Yeah, I baked some chicken and made some vegetables and rice. I'll fix you some."

Kendra headed to the kitchen. Trey got comfortable on the couch and started watching the news. Kendra set up the eating trays, then brought their meals out to the living room.

"What would you like to drink?" she asked as she opened the refrigerator.

"Do you have any of your delicious iced tea made?"

"I sure do, I made it just for you. I knew you'd want some."

"Oh, you knew I'd want some huh?" He laughed.

"Yes, I knew you'd want some tea, so get your mind out of the gutter," she said, laughing with him.

Kendra took a seat next to Trey on the couch, and he said the grace. They were halfway through dinner when a breaking news report came on about a riot at the prison where her father was being held. The report immediately caught Kendra's attention as the news anchor started speaking.

"We're following breaking news right now out of Jessup, Maryland where authorities are on the scene of a violent prison riot involving many of the inmates. Details are still sketchy at this time, but we're told some of the prison guards may have been taken hostage and there are reports of serious injuries. It's unclear at this time just how many inmates are involved, and there's no word as to how many people could be injured. We have a crew on the way and we will continue following this breaking news story to bring you more details as they become available."

"Oh my goodness," Kendra said. "Oh I hope my...uh—" She caught herself before she said *father.*

"Do you know somebody in there?" Trey asked.

"Uh yeah, my, uh, my cousin is in there," she said, looking very nervous. "I should probably go there and make sure he's alright." She got up from the sofa.

"Baby, wait a minute. You can't go running to a prison in the middle of a riot. Now look, just calm down. The best thing you can do is just wait here, continue watching the news, and I'm sure they'll give a phone number or something for family members to call to find out about their loved ones." Trey stood up to comfort her.

As they continued to listen to the news, more reports came in and it sounded more serious by the minute. The news reported that more than thirty people were injured and at least seven people were killed. Kendra was losing it. "I think I should go down there. At least I can find out something."

"Baby, do you know how far Jessup is from here? Besides, the people who work at the prison know that family members are going to be worried, and trust me Kendra, they will provide a phone number or something so people can check on their family members. Baby, you are getting so upset about this. Who is this cousin of yours, how old is he?"

"Trey please, not now, I don't want to get into all of that. Look, I think I should probably be alone so I can call my aunt and cousins and see if they've heard anything."

"Are you sure?"

"Yes, Trey, I'm sure.

"Kendra, promise me you will not leave this house."

"I promise."

When Trey left, Kendra started calling the phone numbers she had to the prison but wasn't getting any answers. She fell to her knees and began to pray.

About three hours later her phone rang. It was someone from the prison telling her that her father had been stabbed during the riot and was in critical condition. They said he was being flown to the Shock Trauma Unit at the University of Maryland Hospital and that she should get there as soon as possible.

♥ *Chapter 30* ♥

When Kendra arrived at the hospital, she learned that her father was in a coma. She was unable to get any other information because the hospital was an absolute madhouse. There were victims from the prison all over the place, and family members screaming and crying. Prison guards and state troopers were all over, patrolling the rooms and the hallways. It looked like a scene from a movie.

Kendra found her father's room and the guard assigned to his room asked her for identification, checked her name on his sheet and allowed her to come in. She sat down in a chair next to his bed and began praying to God that he would pull through.

After about an hour, a nurse came in and checked on Rob.

"Is he going to be okay?" Kendra asked.

"It's hard to say right now. He was seriously injured. Not only did he take a really bad blow to the head, he was also stabbed near his heart," the nurse said.

Kendra broke down and began to cry uncontrollably as the nurse walked out.

What if my father dies, what am I going to do? she thought. She really needed her father. Even though she didn't agree with some of the things he did, she loved him and needed him in her life. She was devastated at the thought of being left in this world with no mother or father.

Kendra sat by her Dad's side for hours. It was hard watching him lie there in a coma. They had handcuffed one of his arms to the bed even though the prison guard was watching his room.

Kendra walked out of the room, hoping to run into someone who could give her some answers about how the riot broke out and exactly what happened to her father. When she walked down the hall she saw Wayne, her father's cellmate, sitting on the side of a bed being examined by a doctor.

"Mr. Wayne," Kendra said as she walked to the door of the room and began to step inside. "Mr. Wayne, are you okay? A guard stepped into her path to keep her from getting too close to Wayne.

"Sir, please, her father is my cellmate and he was hurt really bad in all of this," Wayne said, trying to get the guard to back off and let her talk to him.

The guard backed up slightly and looked up Kendra. "You can talk to him from here, but don't get any closer than this, ma'am," the guard said, watching her every move.

"It's okay, Kendra, the guards and officers have to take extra precautions in situations like this, because a lot of prisoners use hospital visits as an opportunity to escape, and some have friends or family members help them," Wayne said.

"Mr. Wayne, what in the world happened in there?" Kendra asked. She noticed his open wounds and bloody shirt.

"Ah, Kendra, it was a mess, an unbelievable disaster. Some of the inmates got into a huge fight while we were in the yard, then some of the guards stepped in to try and break it up, but they were somehow overpowered, and some of them were taken hostage. Then everybody just went crazy. I think your father was trying to help one of the young guards and got stabbed, then they pushed down and he hit his head on the cement. By the time they got things under control, he had been laying there for a while. The guards had the medical units get him out of there as soon as they could, and I made sure you were one of the ones they notified. It was just crazy. I heard some people were killed, but they haven't told us how many. I'm just glad my injuries are minor, but we're really going to have to pray for your dad, Kendra." Wayne frowned as the doctor probed his injuries, causing him pain.

Kendra stood there in silence, staring at the floor.

"Okay, ma'am, I'm going to have to ask you to leave if you're not family," the guard said, motioning Kendra to the door.

"Mr. Wayne, I'm glad you're okay," Kendra said. She walked out as the tears started.

She walked down the hall, completely dazed, and reached inside her purse for her cell phone. She wanted to call her aunt and tell her what happened, but couldn't find her phone and realized she must have left it in the car. She felt like she didn't have enough energy to go out to the car and get it. Besides, her aunt hated her father. She blamed him for her sister's death. She had always said if he hadn't been accused of rape, her sister would have never been driving home upset and had that terrible accident. She also blamed him for Kendra's sadness because with her sister being gone Kendra no longer had a mother.

Kendra went back into her dad's room. There was still no change. She wished she could get a prognosis on his condition from a doctor, but there was so much chaos in that hospital that she just wanted to sit in the quietness of her father's room.

When Kendra woke up it was after five the next morning. She was hunched over in the same chair she'd been in all night. She looked over at her father. He was still in a coma.

Her body was sore and her neck was stiff. She touched her

father's hand and said another prayer.

After a few minutes, she thought about Trey and hoped he hadn't tried to call her. She didn't want him to worry. Kendra walked to the nurse's station and asked if someone could talk to her about her father's condition. One of the nurses told her the doctor had made his rounds during the night and that another doctor would be making rounds in a couple of hours. She assured Kendra they were keeping a close eye on her dad. The nurse told her she could go home for a while and leave her phone number and that they would call her if there was any change.

Kendra took the nurse's advice and walked to her car. She found her phone on the floor of her car and checked to see if Trey had called. He had tried to call her at eleven o'clock the night before and Kendra hoped that he assumed she was asleep at the time.

Kendra called her job and left a recorded message stating that she wouldn't be in to work.

It took her about 25 minutes to get home from the hospital. Even though she was exhausted, she felt she had to take a shower. By the time she finally made it to her bed, she could hardly keep her eyes open and within minutes she was asleep.

♥ <u>Chapter 31</u> ♥

A couple of hours later the phone rang, waking Kendra out of her sleep. "Hello," she said, barely able to look at the clock.

"Hey baby, this is Trey."

"Hey, Trey."

"Is everything okay? Did you find out anything about your cousin?"

"What?" Kendra replied, caught off guard. She had forgotten that she'd told Trey it was her cousin she was concerned about.

"Your cousin in prison, was he one of the people who got hurt in the riot?"

"Oh, no, no he didn't get hurt." Kendra said, waking up a little more.

"Oh thank God, because I heard more about it on the news, and it was terrible, they said."

"Yeah I know."

"Aren't you going to work today?" Trey asked.

"Oh no, I took off because I have some appointments."

"Oh, okay baby, well, I just wanted to make sure you were

okay. I'm gonna go now because I have a meeting, but I'll call you later."

"Okay Trey, have a good day."

"You too," he said as he hung up the phone.

If only you knew, Trey, there is no way I'm going to have a good day, Kendra thought as she closed her eyes and fell back to sleep.

It was a few minutes after noon when Kendra's cell phone rang, waking her once again. This time it was the hospital.

"Hello," Kendra said.

"Hi, is this Miss Kendra Stewart?"

"Yes it is."

"Hi Miss Stewart, this is Sheila, one of the nurses at University Hospital. I wanted to call to tell you that your father woke up out of the coma and so far seems to be doing a little better."

"Oh, thank you Jesus," Kendra said, with a sigh of relief. "Is he talking and alert?"

"Yes ma'am, he is alert, but he's still being watched very closely by the doctor."

"Can I come to see him?"

"Yes, you sure can."

"Okay, thank you so much for calling me."

"You're quite welcome."

Kendra hung up the phone and immediately fell to her knees in prayer. She thanked God for waking her father out of his coma and asked Him to please let her father make a full recovery. She asked God to heal her relationship with her father. Finally, she asked God to guide her through the process of telling Trey the truth.

When Kendra arrived at the hospital, she noticed how much calmer everything was. She got permission from the nurse's station and the prison guard to go into her father's room. Rob was sleeping when she walked in, but she wanted to make sure that he was really out of the coma, so she tapped him on his arm. After a few taps, Rob started moving his head. Kendra smiled, and then looked up to heaven and whispered, "Thank you, Jesus."

After a few moments Rob opened his eyes. Kendra was standing over him. "Hi Daddy," she said, and she leaned over and kissed his forehead.

"Hey, baby girl," Rob said weakly.

"How do you feel, Daddy?" Kendra pulled a chair up close to the bed.

"I feel like somebody ran over me with a Mack 10," Rob said, trying to smile.

"Do you remember what happened?"

"Yeah, I remember. Everything was crazy. I think it was the second time in my life I was actually scared. I was scared I was never going to see my baby girl again. Baby, I'm so sorry about everything, and I mean *everything.* You didn't deserve the things that happened to you and to our family, and you don't deserve a father who tries to make you do something that's wrong. Oh, baby, I don't know what happened to me to make me such an evil person. Please forgive me." Rob began to cry.

"Oh, Daddy, I forgive you. I love you so much. Don't be so hard on yourself," Kendra said as she wiped her own tears.

"No Kendra, you don't understand. See, I deserved to die in that riot, but I didn't. I used to be a good person and then I just got so full of myself when life was going well for me. I got a little bit of power and didn't know how to act. I used to go to church with you and your mother when you were really young. We were a nice family back then, and I loved your mother. Then I started making a lot of money and I changed. Kendra, I need to tell you the truth."

She wiped the tears from her father's face as he continued. "The truth is I cheated on your mother and at times I hated myself for it, but it seemed like I couldn't stop. I've done a lot of wrong in my life, baby, but I am a good person deep down inside and I want to change. I walk around playing Mr.

Tough Guy, but I'm not. I walk around blaming both the girl who accused me of rape and Tony Boston with ruining my life, when deep down inside I know I ruined my own life, and I felt so bad about it and wanted to get back at Tony, I guess trying desperately to do something to make myself feel better. You know misery loves company."

"It's okay, Daddy," she said, feeling sorry for her father.

"Kendra, when I was laying on that cold cement floor in that prison yard, I thought I was going to die. The sad part is I felt like I deserved to die. I never understood why God let me live and allowed your mother to die when I was the one who did wrong. But when I was lying on that floor, I prayed that God would keep me alive so that I could see you again. Baby, I'm so sorry. Please forgive me," Rob said, reaching for her hand.

"I forgive you, Daddy. I forgave you a long time ago and God forgives you too." Kendra put her hand in his.

"I want to say one more thing. I want to tell you that if you really like Tony's son Trey, then I want you to be happy. I was a fool to ask you to try to get revenge for me. Please do what makes you happy, daughter. God knows life is short, and I can't take anymore of your precious days away from you. So if seeing Trey makes you happy, then that's what I want you to do." Rob smiled at Kendra.

"Daddy, thank you. Thank you so much," Tears poured down Kendra's face.

She sat there with her father for about an hour before the nurse came in and told her she would have to leave so he could rest. Kendra said goodbye to her father and told him she'd be back the next day.

She was so excited that she had her father's blessing to see Trey. Now she wanted to tell Trey the truth so she could finally feel free and they could move on with their relationship, or so she hoped. She decided she would go to his place tonight and tell him.

♥ <u>Chapter 32</u> ♥

*K*im pulled up to the Boston house about 7:30 in the evening. She saw Trey's car in the driveway so she knew he was next door. She assumed Mr. and Mrs. Boston were probably out to dinner since their cars weren't there. She unlocked the door and started to bring in bags of groceries. Kim went back and forth to her car bringing in bags and forgot to lock the front door when she came in the last time.

Once she put everything away she went upstairs to gather the dirty laundry. Kim heard a noise coming out of Trey's old bedroom and went to see what it was. When she walked in the room, she saw Trey walking out of his old bathroom, wrapped in a towel.

"Whoa, what are you doing in here, girl?" Trey said. As he walked into the room, steam came off him.

"Oh sorry, what are you doing in here, Trey?" Kim asked, pleasantly shocked.

"Something's wrong with the hot water next door, and I can't get anybody to come out for a couple of days, so I came over here to take a shower.".

"Oh, okay, well do you have any clothes in here that need to go to the cleaners or down to the laundry,"

"Yeah, you can take all of that over there in the chair. Hey, did things ever calm down at the hospital where you're doing your clinical trials?" he asked.

"Oh, you mean all those patients we got from the prison? Yeah, that was crazy, but things are much calmer. A lot of them were just treated and released. We only kept a few who were seriously injured. All of that confusion had me rethinking my decision to become a nurse. I was thinking that I should have done my clinical trials at the hospital in Howard County instead. But it was good practice for me. The nurses said I needed to experience something like that early on, so that I could be prepared for the worst." Kim got Trey's suit and shirt to add to her basket.

"You're taking a long time getting those clothes. Hurry up and get out of here so I can get dressed.," Trey said laughing.

"Excuse me. You should be thankful that I'm always as helpful as I am. Besides, you know you enjoy my company. Kim smirked.

"Look, just hurry up. I don't feel comfortable being around you with no clothes on. You might try something," Trey said, jokingly.

"I might try something? What about you, like you did before. When we had our so called romantic evening and came close to sleeping with each other." Kim moved a little closer to him.

"Look, Kim that night should have never happened."

"You know what, we need to talk about this, Trey, because we had strong feelings for each other back then and that night happened and we never talked about it. We just walk around like nothing ever happened and that's not cool. I still have feelings for you and you act like you are trying your best not to show that you have feelings for me. Can we talk about this please?" Kim looked into his eyes.

"Okay Kim, look, I did really like you and if you didn't feel like a sister to me, maybe we could have something. But being with you like that felt a little weird. I mean it felt great mentally and emotionally because we get along well and have a lot of fun together. But the romantic part didn't feel right, because you feel like family to me and I don't think I can see myself in a relationship with you. And now I'm in a relationship with someone and I think she might be the one."

"The one what—the one you marry?" Kim asked.

"Yeah, the one I marry."

"Don't you think you're moving a little too fast with this woman? I mean, do you really know her?"

"I know enough to know that I'm on the right track with someone who's good for me. You're not jealous over my relationship with her are you?"

"You should never ask a woman anything like that. But to answer your question, no, I'm not jealous. I just can't help but think that we really could have had something special if you had just given it a chance," She said sadly.

"Given it a chance? Trey shrugged his shoulders.

Kim started getting a little teary- eyed. "Did you ever stop to think that you hurt me?" She turned slightly away so he couldn't see her face.

"Hurt you how?"

Kim started crying. "Trey, I have always liked you and wanted a relationship with you, and then I spent a wonderful night with you that I thought could've been the start of something nice and you act like it meant nothing to you."

"Kim, come on, stop crying. Look, you are a beautiful woman, very intelligent. You'll be finished with school in a few months, you're gonna be one fine nurse…and you're gonna find you somebody nice. What about the student-doctor dude? Are you still seeing him?" Trey moved closer and put his arms around her to comfort her.

Trey and Kim didn't hear Kendra coming up the stairs. She had gone next door to his place, and since Trey wasn't there, she figured he must have been at his Dad's house. When Kendra knocked on the front door it opened because Kim forgot to lock it. Kendra started making her way up the stairs, because she heard voices, and no one answered when she called Trey's name several times. As Kendra got close to the top of the stairs, she heard Kim and Trey talking, and then she could see him standing there in a towel, holding her. Trey was rubbing Kim's face.

"Look, Kim I've always had feelings for you as well and believe it or not, I've thought about what it would have been like if you and I were together. Trey put his hand on Kim's chin to lift her face and kissed her forehead.

When Kendra heard this she ran back down the stairs with tears in her eyes. *He's seeing Kim behind my back! How could he do this to me?* she thought as she ran back out and jumped in her car.

Chapter 33

*K*endra was distraught. It was a wonder she made it back to her apartment. Deep down inside she loved Trey and didn't want to believe he was seeing Kim.

"Trey, how could you do that to me?" she said in a weak voice, as she looked in her bathroom mirror. She kept hearing her father's old words echoing in the back of her mind: *"Tony Boston is a no-good, back-stabbing snake who you can't trust and he probably taught his son to be the same way."* Maybe she should have listened to her father back then. She remembered her father saying something to her a while back. *"Listen to me Kendra, like father, like son, so you can't trust him. Tony Boston destroyed our family and made it impossible for us to have a good life and I need you to help me pay them back."*

"No," she screamed. She lightly hit her head on the mirror. "Oh God, help me. I feel so confused. I think Trey loves me. It's probably just that Kim came on to him, that's all. She's probably been throwing herself at him for years. He doesn't love her, he doesn't want her. He loves me, he wants me. What am I going to do?"

After a while she felt as if she was numb. She was starting

to think that her emotional and nervous systems were shutting down because of all the pain. She took some medicine for her headache, turned both her cell phone and home phone off so she wouldn't be tempted to answer Trey's call and went to bed. She just needed to sleep and forget as much as possible. She needed a break from it all.

Kendra tried desperately to fall sleep but tossed and turned all night. She started having bad dreams.

In the first dream, she was sitting in the prison waiting room with tears in her eyes waiting for her father. Rob came out and immediately saw that she was upset. He reached over and hugged her. "What's the matter, what is it, baby?"

"Oh Daddy, you were right." Kendra could no longer keep the tears from falling. "Daddy, I started writing you a letter at first but then I just had to come down here because I felt so terrible. See, at first I wanted to do what you wanted me to do and help you get even with Mr. Boston and destroy his family like he destroyed ours. But then I met him and his family and I thought they were really nice people. And I started falling in love with Trey and he was the best man I'd ever met in my life, until—" She paused because she was crying so hard she could barely get her words out.

"Until what, baby," Rob asked.

"Until I saw him in the arms of another woman. I think he's been cheating on me the whole time, and I think they had just finished being romantic when I saw them together in his bedroom."

Rob sat quietly like he wanted to speak but something was weighing his tongue down. "Kendra, how could you allow yourself to fall for this man? Didn't I make it very clear to you that Tony Boston was a double-crossing, no-good punk who didn't care about anybody but himself. He obviously raised his son to be just like him. Like father like son, and now like father like daughter. I want you to do what we planned to do from the beginning. Bring Tony Boston and his family down to their knees and make sure you mess them up real bad. They're gonna pay for all the years they put me in here. You must find a way to cause separation between Tony and his son like my going to jail caused separation between me and my child, you understand me?" Rob said angrily as he grabbed Kendra by the shoulders and shook her.

Kendra just nodded her head yes and wiped her tears. "I hate him now, Daddy, don't worry, I see right through that no good two-timer, and I believe that Tony double-crossed you when he was supposed to be defending you as your lawyer. Don't worry, I'll get them, the whole family and that sneaky housekeeper." Kendra had a faraway look in her eyes, almost like she was another person.

Kendra abruptly woke up out of the dream. *Thank God that was just a dream,* she thought. She turned and looked at the clock. It was 4:30 in the morning. She rubbed her head and started crying. *My mind is playing tricks on me,* she thought as she cried herself back to sleep.

Kendra abruptly woke up out of another dream a few hours later. She stared at the ceiling for a few minutes, then glanced at the clock and panicked when she saw it was 9:30 in the morning. She thought she was late for work but then remembered it was Saturday.

Kendra felt as if she had the weight of the world on her shoulders and almost as if she didn't want to get out of bed and face another day. She reached for her Bible on the nightstand. Her mother always told her when she felt depressed, or during devastating times when she felt like she was at the absolute end of her rope, to always pick up her Bible and turn to one of her favorite verses. Her mother told her to remember to hold on to her faith and that God doesn't put any more on us than we can handle. He knows exactly what He's doing at all times. She told her to never, ever give up and not to ever lose hope or faith. When Kendra found her favorite verse in the Bible, she read it aloud several times. She then sat quietly on the bed. Even though she felt devastated, deep down inside, she was still holding on to her faith and hope, just like her Mom always told her to do.

About an hour later Kendra took a shower and made a cup of tea. As she sat at the kitchen table, she decided she needed to reach out to somebody. She was so disappointed that when she went to Trey's house to finally tell him the truth about her past, she discovered some untruth about him and his obvious relationship with Kim.

Kendra felt like she could talk to Miss Sheila. She knew that she could open up to her about everything, including her past and about what she saw between Trey and Kim. She called the spa and made a same-day appointment with Miss Sheila. Then she got on her knees and prayed for God to order her steps. She would go to the spa right after she visited her father in the hospital. She needed relief. She needed to come clean. She needed a mother figure to talk to, and today, she needed Miss Sheila.

♥ _Chapter 34_ ♥

When Kendra walked into the hospital room, she was surprised to see her father looking much better. His complexion looked good and he was more alert. "Hey there, baby girl," Rob said.

"Hey there, Pops," she said as she hugged him.

"Did you call me Pops? Oh goodness, I must be looking bad or looking old." He laughed.

"You don't look old or bad at all; in fact, you're looking much stronger.

Kendra noticed that there was another patient in the room with her father, but the curtain was pulled shut. She could also tell there were a couple of nurses on that patient's side of the room. What she didn't know was that one of the nurses was actually training a nursing student, and that student was Kim.

"So did you take my advice about going after what makes you happy, Kendra?" her father asked.

"Well, let's just say that I plan to follow my heart, Daddy," she replied.

"You know, to be honest with you, if Trey is anything like his father, then he's a good guy. The more I think about it, the more upset I am with myself for telling you to set them up to take a fall. I'm glad I came to my senses, or rather, I'm glad that God brought me to my senses and made me see the light. You're a good girl, Kendra, and truly a Godsend. If Trey does end up with you, he's gonna be one lucky man. You just tell that Boston boy he'd better treat you like the princess you are." Rob smiled at his daughter.

Kim heard everything that was said and couldn't believe her ears. She recognized Kendra's voice and could not believe that this man was talking about how Kendra was supposed to set up Tony and Trey Boston to take a fall. Kim had to tell the Boston family about this, but first she had to find out this man's identity. *How am I going to get out of the room without Kendra seeing me?* she thought.

When the nurse finished with the other patient, she slid the curtain back. As she did this, Kim put the patient's chart on the side of her face to hide from Kendra and walked out of the room. Kendra and Rob never noticed a thing.

Kim walked over to the nurse's station to look for the name of the patient. It was listed as Robert Stewart—Prison Inmate. *Oh my goodness, what in the world is going on?* she thought. She had to warn Trey and his parents.

Kendra stayed in the room with her father for about an hour then told him to get some rest. She left the hospital and drove to the spa to see Miss Sheila.

♥ <u>Chapter 35</u> ♥

*T*rey was surprised that he hadn't heard back from Kendra after leaving her a message last night. He wanted to set up a romantic date with her at a nice restaurant because he was on a mission. He went to his parents' jewelers and picked out an engagement ring so he could propose to her.

He'd been eyeing the ring for a couple of weeks and made sure all of his C's were in order: carat, cut, color, and clarity. He had learned a lot about purchasing jewelry from his mom. Trey had also done his research. After all, he was a lawyer and a very smart guy. Once he was finished in the store he headed straight home. Little did he know a bomb was about to explode in his life.

Kendra arrived at the spa at 1:30 on the dot for her appointment with Miss Sheila. She signed in and took a seat. The receptionist sent some kind of electronic signal to Sheila's massage room to let her know that her next appointment had arrived. A few minutes later, Sheila came to the front to get Kendra.

"Hello, Kendra," she said with a big smile.

"Hi, Miss Sheila," Kendra said as she opened her arms to give her a hug.

Kendra always felt so calm and safe around Miss Sheila. It was probably because she was a wise woman with a calm and gentle spirit.

"Come on back, sweetie. You're my last client so I can really take my time with you." She motioned Kendra to follow her.

By the time they got to the back, Kendra's eyes were filled with tears. Everything was so overwhelming for her, from lying to Trey, to meeting Rhonda, to her father almost getting killed, and then to top it off, to suspect Trey of being involved with Kim.

"You can put your things here in the cabinet, Kendra." When Kendra didn't respond, Sheila turned to look at her.

"Sweetie, are you okay?" Sheila asked when she saw Kendra's tears, which had started streaming down her face at that very moment.

"Miss Sheila, I really need to talk to you." Kendra sat down.

"Sure, what is it?" Sheila asked, sitting down beside Kendra on the soft love seat.

"I don't know where to begin. This is all going to sound so bizarre, but I don't know who else to turn to."

"Okay, come on, just take your time. Talk to me." Sheila put her arm around Kendra to console her.

"Miss Sheila, there is a lot going on and I need your help. First of all, I want you to know that I am really in love with Trey. He is the absolute best thing that has ever happened to me and I already know that I want to spend the rest of my life with him. But I met Trey under false pretenses. My name isn't really Kendra Jackson, it's Kendra Stewart. Jackson is the last name of my mother's sister, and I started using that name after my mother died and my father went to jail. The reason I never told Trey my real name was because of my past and what my father wanted me to do. You see, my father's name is Rob Stewart. He was friends with you and Mr. Tony in college and he was later accused of raping one of his students when he was a college professor."

Sheila cut in. "I know who Rob Stewart is. Are you saying he is your father and your mother was the woman who was killed in the car accident?"

Sheila looked puzzled.

"Yes, Miss Sheila, but please don't be mad at me, please hear me out." Kendra continued. "My father has always blamed Mr. Tony for his being in prison. He said that Mr. Tony did not defend him properly on purpose because he wanted to see him go to jail. My father said he thought that Mr. Tony turned against him and started believing the girl who was accusing him of rape. My father has been in jail for twelve years, and during that entire time he has been telling me that he wanted Tony Boston to pay for what he had done to him. My father blames himself for my mother's death. He said that if he had not been accused of rape, then she would still be alive.

"A couple of months before I met Trey, my father became really depressed in prison. At that time, he made me promise to help him get back at Mr. Tony by causing some type of public embarrassment to him and his family. He never talked about anything violent, he just wanted me to get close to Trey and then somehow cause trouble for the family. I never wanted to do it and never intended to do it, and the only reason I set out to meet Trey was because he kept pressuring me about it. I only said I would do it so that he wouldn't be so depressed. I am a Christian woman who loves God with all my heart, and I would never do anything to hurt anyone. I was just trying to appease my father by saying okay. I was gonna tell him that I met Trey and that he was not interested in me and then leave the whole thing alone." Kendra wiped her eyes as her tears slowed.

She continued. "The problem is, I ended up taking a real liking to Trey and wanted to be around him more and more. I still never intended to do any of the things my father was asking. The more time Trey and I spent together, the more I wanted to be with him, and soon things had gone too far and I didn't know how to tell him about my true identity. I also fell in love with you, Mr. Tony, and Todd. You all were so wonderful to me and made me feel like part of the family. It felt so good to have that and I just couldn't say or do anything to hurt you all.

"I guess I was just secretly hoping my bad past would vanish and I could go on with life with you guys, but my guilt was eating me up and I had to tell Trey. Last night I went to his place to talk to him about all of this, but instead I found him in your house, upstairs in his bedroom with Kim."

"What? Trey and Kim in the bedroom? I mean, what were they doing?" Miss Sheila seemed almost afraid of the answer.

Kendra's eyes began to fill with tears again. "I believe there was something going on, like they had just finished making love. They didn't hear me come in because someone had left the front door unlocked and when I knocked it came open. I was calling Trey's name but he couldn't hear me. But I knew someone was there because both their cars were in the driveway. When I walked upstairs, I saw him with nothing on but a towel. He was holding Kim, rubbing her face and looking into her eyes." Kendra started sobbing and Miss Sheila handed her some tissue.

"Trey was talking about his feelings for her. I didn't want them to hear me crying so I ran out of the house. I just wanted to tell him the truth and tell him that my father is sorry for everything and admits that he was wrong for asking me to do something like that. See, my father was one of the inmates hurt in that big prison riot last week. He's fortunate to be alive right now because he was stabbed near his heart. I know it was nothing but the grace of God that kept him alive. I also know it was God's will to break him so that he would change his ways. Miss Sheila, I have been walking around with all this on me for so long because I just didn't have anyone I could talk to."

"Oh, you poor thing. I am so sorry you had to go through all of this. I know you are a sweet person and wouldn't do anything to hurt Trey or any of us. You didn't have to be afraid to tell us. I really wish you had come to me sooner, so I could've helped you." Sheila hugged her tightly.

"You know something that was also eating away at me was the fact that I met the young lady who said my father raped her and I believe her. She also told me that there were rumors that my father had slept with some of the students on campus. My father just admitted to me that he cheated on my mom," Kendra said and cried like a baby. Sheila started crying along with her because she could see that she was in so much pain and was being honest about everything.

"Look at me, Kendra. "I am going to help you. We'll talk to Trey together. He will forgive you for not being honest with him about your past. As for the rest of us, trust me, we all love you, sweetie. Besides, I am a very discerning woman. I can see you have a genuine heart. I can also see that you really love my son. As far as the part about him and Kim, I honestly don't believe that anything was going on with those two. I think you may have walked in on a conversation they may have been having about something that happened in the past. Trey is crazy about you and my son seems to be a one-woman man. But that's something that the two of you will have to work out. I am not going to get into that. I will, however, help you explain all this other stuff to him."

"Thank you so much, Miss Sheila. I prayed to God for someone I could look up to like a Mom, and I know that you are that answered prayer," Kendra said, trying to smile.

"You're welcome, sweetie. Now, tell me, what are the doctors saying about your father? Is he going to be okay?"

"Yes, they expect him to make a full recovery. They said he should be released in about a week."

Kendra and Sheila decided to reschedule the appointment. Kendra said she wanted to go home and change and then come to the house later so they could talk to Trey together.

♥ <u>Chapter 36</u> ♥

Trey walked into the house looking like he was having one of the best days of his life. His father was sitting in the family room watching college football on the big screen television.

"Whassup, Dad?" Trey said when he walked into the room.

"Hey there, son," Tony replied.

"Who's winning?" Trey took a seat in the reclining leather sectional sofa.

"Man, Penn State is killing Ohio State right now," Tony said, just as a commercial came on. Trey used this opportunity to pull the engagement ring out of the bag and show it to his father.

"Check this out, Dad," he said as he passed the box over to his father.

Tony looked surprised when Trey handed him the ring box and almost hesitated when accepting it. "Whoa, son, is this what I think it is?"

"Yep, sure is. I'm gonna pop the question tonight."

"Wow, this is beautiful. I knew you were crazy about her and you told me you thought she was the one, but this is a little soon, isn't it?"

"Well, it's been about six months, and we don't have to set a date right now. I just know that she's the one. I love her." Trey smiled.

"Well then, son, do your thing and follow your heart. Just one piece of advice, don't move too fast with the marriage date. Set a wedding date far enough in advance so that you can make sure it's right, okay?"

"Okay, Dad." Trey went to the kitchen to get something to drink.

About an hour later Kim came in the door. She looked frazzled.

"Are you okay?" Tony asked.

"No, I'm not. Trey, I really need to talk to you," she said, looking at Trey with panic.

"What is it, Kim?" Trey asked.

"It's about Kendra!"

"What happened to Kendra?" Trey asked as he stood up. He looked like he was afraid of the words that were about to come out of Kim's mouth.

"Nothing happened to her. I just found out something about her that I think you should know, but I don't know if I should tell you in front of your father."

"You can say anything in front of my father. We don't have any secrets in this house."

"Okay, when I was at the hospital today, Kendra was there visiting one of those patients from the jail, and I heard her calling him Daddy. When I checked the charts I saw that his name was Robert Stewart and that he was from the prison. When Kendra was in the room with him he was saying things like she was supposed to do something to bring Tony Boston and his son down."

Trey and Tony sat there in silence, both with a puzzled look on their face.

"Kim, are you sure this happened? I mean, this doesn't make sense," Trey said, looking completely baffled.

"Yes it does," Tony said. "Rob Stewart is the man I represented in the only case I ever lost. He used to write me letters from prison saying that he would get revenge on me. Oh, Trey, I am so sorry," Tony said. He stood up, shaking his head.

"This is crazy. Kim, are you saying that the only reason she was with me was so that she could help her father get back at my father?" Trey looked like he was about to cry.

"Yes, Trey, that's exactly what I heard. I'm sorry that I had to be the one to tell you. I feel terrible and I didn't want to hurt you, but I had to tell you. I'm not going to let anyone hurt this family," Kim said.

"It's not your fault, Kim." Tony said.

"Damn it! What the hell is going on?" Trey yelled. He threw the ring box across the room. Tony walked over to him.

"Son, it's okay, we'll get to the bottom of this."

"This is so messed up, Dad. I love that woman, what the hell am I supposed to do now?" Trey stormed out of the house.

"Trey, wait," Kim and Tony yelled as they both ran behind him. Trey ignored them. He then jumped into his car and peeled out of the driveway.

♥ <u>Chapter 37</u> ♥

Kendra was feeling better after her talk with Miss Sheila. She was at home about to take a shower when the doorbell rang. She became a little nervous because she wasn't expecting anyone. She then figured it was Trey because she had turned both of her phones off and he was probably trying to reach her. She slipped her robe over her naked body and tiptoed to the door. She looked through the peephole and saw Trey. She opened the door. Trey stormed in.

"Trey, what's wrong?" she asked looking nervous.

"What's wrong? You don't know what's wrong? Your little cover is blown. That's what's wrong. From what I hear, you're the daughter of Rob Stewart, who doesn't live in Illinois, like you said your father did. No, your father lives in jail. Your father told you to get next to me so you could help him hurt my family. Was that your plan, Kendra? Were you supposed to hurt me and my family? Was everything we had a lie Kendra? Did I fall in love with a woman who was plotting something against me and my family?"

Trey paced back and forth, yelling in her face and not allowing her to get a word in. "You're quite an actress you know that."

Kendra started crying and yelling as she tried to get him to hear her. "No, Trey you're wrong!" she said as she tried to touch him.

"Don't touch me," he yelled as he pushed her arms away. "What, was Kim telling a lie? She saw you at hospital, Kendra. She heard you and your father talking, Kendra. She's a student at that hospital. So was she lying or are you the liar?" Trey said, walking over to her.

Kendra's robe came open as she tried to grab Trey. When he saw her naked body, he grabbed her by the arms. "Was it all a lie, Kendra?" Trey yanked off her robe and pulled her back to the bedroom.

"You wanted to get next to me to get back at my father. Now I'm gonna get next to you to get back at your father." Trey threw her on the bed.

"No, Trey, please stop!" She screamed and cried.

He started unbuckling his pants.

"Trey, please don't do this. I love you so much. I was never going to hurt you. Please talk to your mother. She knows all about it. I told her everything and she believed me. I love you—please don't hurt me!" Kendra tried desperately to fight Trey off, but he was too strong.

"Shut up," Trey said as he slid his pants down and got on top of her.

"Trey, please don't do this to me. I love you, I was not going to go through with it. Please believe me. You know I love God too much to do anything like that," Kendra said as she continued to fight him.

Trey stopped when she mentioned how much she loved God, because so did he and he knew that this was not of God. He let go of the tight grip he had on her wrists and rolled off of her. He then got off the bed, leaned back against the wall and started crying. "How could you do this to me, Kendra? I can't even look at you anymore. I really loved you. Now I don't ever want to lay eyes on you again. You hear me? Stay the hell away from me, Kendra."

With that Trey hung his head and walked out. She stayed on the bed crying and then heard her front door slam behind him. "Oh God help me!" she screamed.

Sheila pulled up to the Boston house and noticed Tony and Kim leaning against Kim's car talking. She saw the look of concern on their faces, which in turn concerned her. Tony walked over to open the door for his wife.

"Tony, is everything okay?" Sheila asked as she stepped out of the car.

"No, it's not, baby," Tony said as he closed the door.

"What is it?" Sheila asked, looking at the both of them.

"Come on in the house, baby, you need to sit down for this one."

The three of them walked into the kitchen and sat down.

"Sheila, I don't know where to start," he said.

Kim jumped in. "It's all my fault, Miss Sheila."

"No it's not, Kim. I told you to stop blaming yourself," Tony said.

"Would somebody please tell me what's going on," Sheila said, looking frustrated.

Tony started explaining. "Kim found out something very disturbing about Kendra. She's Rob Stewart's daughter. You know, Rob Stewart, the college professor who went to jail for raping one of his—"

Sheila shook her head as she interrupted Tony. "I know all about it."

"What?" Tony and Kim said in unison.

"Kendra and I had a long talk at the spa today. She broke down and told me everything. I told her that I would talk to her and Trey about it so that things wouldn't get of control. I guess she decided to tell him on her own. Where is Trey now?" Sheila asked, calm but concerned.

"Well, that's the thing. We can't find Trey. He stormed out of the house and won't answer his cell phone. Plus Kendra isn't the one who told Trey about her father, I did," Kim said, looking as if she felt like the worse person in the world.

"You did? How did you know about this?"

"I heard them together at the hospital and I came home and told Trey."

"Oh Kim, I wish you would have talked to me first. What did Trey say when he left?"

"Baby, he was furious. He really didn't say anything. He just flew out of here. The sad thing about it all is that he bought the girl an engagement ring today and told me that he loved her. He showed me the ring right before Kim told us everything," Tony said, shaking his head.

Kim looked shocked when she heard about the ring.

"Okay, I'm going to help them fix this. That girl really loves Trey and she is so ashamed about all of this. We all need to pray right now for both of them," Sheila said as she reached for both their hands to pray, something they did whenever they faced obstacles.

♥ <u>Chapter 38</u> ♥

*T*wo days passed and Kendra hadn't heard a word from Trey. She'd called Sheila several times and was told no one had heard from him. Kendra told Miss Sheila how furious Trey was when he came to her apartment.

As more time passed, everyone became increasingly worried because Trey wasn't answering his phone. Sheila told Kendra to keep praying and having faith and that God was going to make everything right.

Kendra sat on the sofa, looking at the flyer of the house that she and Trey fell in love with when they went house hunting. She had actually hoped one day they would move into that house together, but things looked hopeless now.

A few hours later, Kendra's phone rang and she picked it up immediately, hoping it was Trey.

"Hey, baby girl," her father said.

"Hey, Daddy," Kendra said, sounding pitiful.

"I got some really good news, Kendra."

"Oh yeah, I could certainly use some of that."

"Are you okay?" Rob asked.

"Yeah, I just don't feel well right now, but I'll be okay." She just didn't have the mental or emotional energy to go into everything that had happened between her and Trey.

"Have you been to the doctor?"

"It's nothing serious, Daddy, I just have a headache. Nothing a little rest won't take care of."

"Okay, baby. Well, I'll tell you my good news real fast and let you get some rest. You won't believe this. A couple of the officials from the prison came to visit me at the hospital today. They said it was an amazing and heroic thing that I did when I helped to save that prison guard's life. They said they're reducing my sentence for good behavior, so instead of having to serve the last thirteen months of my sentence, I only have to do two more months, and they're dropping the rest." Rob sounded as excited as he could be.

"Oh Daddy, that is so great! Oh, God is so good," Kendra said.

"I know. When they told me that, I couldn't believe it, and I promise you that we're gonna make up for lost time. I'm gonna be a good father to you and a changed man, Kendra, you'll see," Rob said sincerely.

"Okay, Daddy, and I'm sorry that I haven't been to see you these last two days. Hopefully, I'll be able to make it to the hospital tomorrow."

"Well, the doctors said they're releasing me soon, so make sure you call the hospital first to see if I'm still here."

"Okay, I will."

"Alright, baby, get some rest and get better. I love you."

"I love you too, Daddy."

Trey pulled up to his parents' house about ten o'clock Monday morning. He noticed his mother's car was there and was glad she was home. He really needed to talk to her now that he'd had his cooling off period. He felt so hurt, so devastated, and things just didn't make sense.

"Ma, where are you?" Trey yelled as he walked into the house.

"Trey, is that you?" Sheila yelled from the top of the stairs. She came running downstairs and hugged him as tight as she could.

"Trey, are you okay? Where have you been? We were so worried," Sheila said with tears in her eyes. The puffiness around her eyes was a sure sign that she'd been doing a lot of crying.

"Mom, I'm fine. I didn't mean to worry everybody, but I just had to get away."

He told his mother he'd checked into a hotel and spent most of the time thinking and praying. "I just feel like crap, Mom, like the biggest dummy in the world. I feel like I got played in the worst way. Not for money or anything, but so that somebody could try to hurt my family. The whole thing just blows me away." Trey hung his head.

"Son, sit down." She pulled out two chairs at the table, and they both took a seat. "Trey, listen to me carefully. Kendra is a genuine girl and is truly in love with you."

"Ma, how can you say that? Didn't Dad tell you what happened?"

"Trey, hear me out, please, and don't interrupt. You have to hear this. Kendra came to me early Saturday afternoon, the same day Kim told you about what happened. Only Kendra didn't know that Kim saw her at the hospital. She came to me because she wanted to tell me everything and wanted to know how she could tell you. That girl loves you, Trey. She had tried to tell you a couple of days before, but she saw you and Kim in each other's arms upstairs in your old bedroom, and she said you were wrapped in a towel. Trey, she thinks you're sleeping with Kim."

Trey and his Mom talked for two hours about everything. By the time they were finished, Trey saw things in a totally different light. His mother helped him to see that Kendra had been intimated and manipulated by her father for years. His mother also helped him to realize how much Kendra really loved him and that it was just a coincidence that Kim saw her on the same day that she came to the spa. Trey explained why he was in a towel hugging Kim.

After they talked, Sheila called Tony, Kim, and Kendra to let them know that Trey was home and safe. Kendra asked if she could speak to him, but Sheila told her that he would call her back. Trey asked his Mom to pray with him. He then called his secretary and told her he wouldn't be in and gave her a few instructions.

Trey then took a shower and got dressed. He called Kendra and told her he didn't want to get into anything over the phone but that they needed to talk and asked if he could come over. Kendra started crying.

"Yes, Trey, you can come over."

"I'll see you soon, Kendra."

It was about three o'clock when Trey knocked on Kendra's door. She opened it immediately. As soon as they made eye contact, they fell into each other's arms as if a super-strength magnet had pulled them together. Kendra was overwhelmed with emotion as tears soon found their way to her bloodshot, puffy eyes.

Without saying a word, Trey took her hand and led her over to the couch. Kendra could see tears in Trey's eyes as he started to speak. He explained why finding out about her past from Kim was a total shock and why it hurt so much. He avoided bringing up the subject of the ring.

As they talked, Kendra went through the entire story that she'd told his mother. There was so much pain coming out of her that Trey's heart was feeling some of it for her. It was like an emotional explosion.

After Kendra stopped talking about her father and her past, Trey addressed the situation about Kim being in his room. He explained how there was nothing to it and told Kendra that he would never cheat on her.

Trey then touched Kendra's face and looked into her eyes,

"Baby, I'm so sorry for how I treated you the other day. I just felt like I was going crazy, and I'm so sorry that I attacked you like that. I will never try to force myself on you ever again. It's just that I felt like everything had been snatched away from me. You didn't deserve that baby. I want to be gentle with you. I love you." With that Trey kissed Kendra,

"I love you too, Trey."

♥ Chapter 39 ♥

Over the next couple of days, Kendra thought about how happy she was that life was going so well. As she was dressing for work one morning, she paused to smile at her reflection in the mirror, something she couldn't have fathomed a little while ago. She then looked to heaven and smiled as her way of recognizing that it was God who made everything better and she was thankful that things were really starting to come together. She and Trey had reconciled and life was great. Her father was out of the hospital and back in prison, finishing out the last two months of his reduced sentence.

Kendra felt as if things she'd been praying about for years were finally starting to come to fruition. She'd been praying to God asking that He would fix her father's heart and make him a more loving person and that he'd repent. She'd been praying that God would order her steps and send her a good, Christian man who knew how to love her because he first knew how to love God. She'd been asking God for a mother figure who could help her feel the kind of motherly love she so desperately missed, and now she had Miss Sheila.

Kendra knew she owed it all to God and that she was

nothing without Him.

When Kendra arrived at work, she received a call from Trey asking if she'd like to have dinner later that night. They agreed to meet at one of the steakhouses downtown.

Their dinner was delicious. Trey had a steak and Kendra had seafood. They sat and talked for about twenty minutes and then took a nice ride to Washington, D.C. Once there, they parked and took a stroll around the water.

Trey reached for Kendra's hand and turned her around to face him. "Kendra, I'm ready to start moving forward in my life in a lot of ways, and I know that I can't accomplish anything without God. I believe God has brought us together and I want to make it official. You know, I look at my parents and they are such a wonderful example of the type of life I want to have. I want to be a man just like my father. I mean, he had his fun in college with the ladies before he met my mom and everything, but since they got married, he told me that he's been all about her and that was the only woman he needed. He said God blessed him with his queen, and that he always wanted to treat her as such."

Tears came to Kendra's eyes. "That's so beautiful. I wish my father could have been more like yours. He just messed everything up and hurt my mom so much."

"Hey, come here. Part of living the way God wants us to means forgiving others. You have got to find it in your heart to really forgive your father deep down. Kendra, nobody is perfect, we all mess up every now and then. But you have to look at the good in people because there is good in everyone. Look at the fact that your father was good to her for a lot of those years, as you said before. Look at the fact that he was a great provider and a good father to you. I mean, you said that you all had a great family life for a while. Plus he told you when he was in the hospital that he wanted to be a better person, so forgive him deep down and not just on the surface, and then help him to become that better person. Keep praying for your father."

"You're right, Trey, thanks. They smiled at each other and shared a kiss.

As they continued walking, Trey thought about the engagement ring he'd bought before all the drama started. He decided to wait a little while before he proposed.

♥ <u>Chapter 40</u> ♥

*S*heila was in the kitchen when the phone rang.

"Hello."

"Hey Ma, guess what?" Todd yelled through the phone.

"Todd, hey baby," she said, happy to hear from her baby boy.

"Ma, I just met Barack Obama! He came to Atlanta and gave a campaign speech. Ma, it was so uplifting and inspiring and I really felt moved. You know, he just makes me feel like things could be much better in the world if we had leaders who really cared and I want to help him become our next president. I signed up to become a volunteer with his campaign and I'm going to get as many people to vote for him as I can. I mean, so many different people were there from all races and all ages. People are crazy about that man. Plus, you know Atlanta already has so much history with Martin Luther King, Jr., memories and movements and all the civil rights leaders here. It's just incredible, Mom," Todd said, almost all in one breath.

"Todd, I am so proud of you, son. To be so young, you really are an amazing young man. I am so proud that you want to take part in helping Barack Obama become president, and not only become president, but to make history. We need him so much in the White House, not just because it's about time an African American was in the White House, but because of everything that he stands for."

"I know, Ma, he's just so awesome. I was able to take a picture with him. I'll email it to you."

"Okay, son, hold on—your father wants to speak to you."

"Hey Todd," Tony said as he took the phone.

"Hey Dad, guess what, I met Barack Obama."

"So I heard."

"I took a picture with him and I signed up to be a volunteer for his campaign."

"Wow man, that's great. We really need him in office, so that's really good, man. I'm proud of you," Tony said, grinning from ear to ear.

Trey and Kim were both at the house and also had a chance to talk to Todd. They were all very proud of what he'd just done.

Kendra was home in her bed talking to Trey on the phone. They usually talked every night before going to sleep. She told him that she was planning to go see her father on Sunday and asked if he would go with her. Trey was taken back a bit, because he didn't know how her father would react to him. Things were going so well between he and Kendra and he didn't want to have to deal with any more drama. Plus sometimes Kendra had a tendency to get excited and try to rush things along instead of letting them happen naturally. He wanted to think about it for a while, but Kendra was trying to push him for a yes answer right away. Trey thought he should talk to his father about it first. He really didn't know a lot about the man, but his father did.

Trey asked why he couldn't just meet her father when he came home from prison, but Kendra was insistent on Trey meeting him in there. She said her father felt ashamed to be in prison and that she was the only one who'd ever visited him. She thought if Trey went with her, it would help to restore some of her father's dignity. She thought that if he felt like someone else cared enough to actually come to the prison to meet him, then that would do so much for his self-esteem. Kendra had tried for years to tell her father that being in prison wasn't the end of the world and it wasn't a permanent stamp that meant you were nothing. She also told him that many of the great men in the Bible were in prison at one time. She was in no way trying to say that going to jail was acceptable, and that it was alright to commit a crime. The point she was trying to get across to him was that when we fall down, we can't stay down. That when we fall down, we can't get down on ourselves, and when we're already down, we can't look down, because at that point the only other direction to look is up.

She wanted Trey to see that her father was a good man who'd made some terrible mistakes. She wanted to know that Trey would and could accept her father no matter what the circumstance. Kendra knew that Trey and her Dad would like one another. Her father had changed so much after being in the hospital. Plus she wanted her father to see that Trey was a great guy.

Trey told Kendra he would think about it and let her know if he would go with her.

♥ ♥ ♥ ♥ ♥ ♥ ♥ ♥ ♥ ♥ ♥ ♥ ♥ ♥ ♥ ♥ ♥ ♥ ♥

Trey and Kendra went to the early service at church on Sunday, so they could visit her father afterward. Kendra was so excited that he'd agreed to go. Trey wanted to make her happy and asked his father's advice on the situation. Tony told Trey he didn't think there was anything wrong with it. He also told him to take it easy when he met Rob and to just be himself.

Tony said it probably wouldn't be a good idea to bring him up unless Rob specifically asked about Trey's parents. He told Trey to be honest with Rob about his feelings for Kendra. He advised him not to shock him by saying he was ready to propose to her, but said he should let Rob know that he hoped that maybe one day he and Kendra could take things to the next level.

As Trey and Kendra rode to the prison, they really didn't talk much. Both of them seemed to be lost in their own thoughts.

Once they arrived, Kendra introduced Rob and Trey. Trey was surprised at how much Kendra looked like her father, but at the same time she looked a lot like the photo of her mother that she previously showed him. Rob was also surprised at how much Trey looked liked Tony.

Rob and Trey seemed to hit it off, much to Kendra's liking. They talked and joked and had a great conversation. They even talked about the Lord, which made Kendra very happy. She could truly see that her father was a different man.

The next day Trey talked to his parents and told them all about his visit with Rob. He told them that Rob had asked about both of them and wanted Trey to tell them hello. Tony and Sheila thought that was very nice and were both happy to hear that the visit went well.

Trey then told his parents that he was ready to propose to Kendra. They were glad to hear the two of them were working things out and that Trey was ready to take the next step. Sheila said she thought Kendra would make a great wife and a good mother and that she was glad he was making this move because she was ready for some grandchildren. Tony agreed with her.

A few days after he talked to his parents, Trey started thinking about how to propose to Kendra. He called and made dinner reservations at a fancy restaurant in D.C. He then started thinking about how he wanted to present the ring to her. He first thought about having the chef put the ring in a covered dish. Then he thought about slipping it in her glass, but he was scared she might swallow it and choke. He thought about slipping it down her blouse, but thought he might get slapped.

He then thought about putting it on the end of her fork so that when she went to put the food in her mouth, it would bling in her face. But he figured that wouldn't work, because she liked to eat so much, and she'd probably stuff the ring in her mouth with the food.

Trey didn't know how he was going to propose, so he called Sean and Joe. He figured once they got over the initial shock of hearing the news that he was getting hitched, they could help him brainstorm. He knew they would come up with some crazy, off the wall suggestions.

The guys met at a sports bar downtown. As they were waiting for the waitress to bring their food, Trey broke the news.

"Look, check this out: I'm about to ask Kendra to marry me and I want y'all to help me come up with a plan on how to give her the ring." He said it kind of nonchalantly, hoping he wouldn't catch too much crap from them.

Sean acted like he was choking on his beer. "What did you just say, man?"

"You heard me. I said I am about to propose to Kendra. You know, ask her to marry me. Ask if he she will become my wife." Trey smirked.

"Man, why do you wanna go and do a thing like that?" Sean

asked, shaking his head in disbelief.

"Leave him alone, Sean. If he wants to give up his freedom and mess up our little trio, then let him go right ahead," Joe said, shrugging his shoulders.

"Look, forget y'all. I know what's good for me and I really feel like she's the one and I'm ready to get married." Trey held his bottle of beer up as if he wanted to toast.

Sean and Joe looked around as if trying to ignore Trey's notion.

"Man look, I know she's fine and I know you say she's smart and a good girl and all, but seriously, you haven't been seeing her long enough to get married," Joe said.

"Look man, it's been about eight months now and I said I'm gonna propose to her, I didn't say we were about to walk down the aisle. I want to wait a while for that, but I'm ready to propose to her. I know what I want and she fits the bill. And don't worry, my getting engaged won't change a thing. We'll still be able to hang out and everything else."

"Yeah, right. I'm telling you now, if I see you getting henpecked, I'm gonna call you out," Sean said. They all laughed.

After going back and forth and joking with Trey for about forty-five minutes, Sean and Joe finally told him that they were really happy for him. They celebrated with a toast.

Trey asked his buddies to help him find a unique way to propose. Sean laughed and said he had an idea.

"Okay, here it is," Sean said as he prepared them for the ultimate perfect proposal.

"You two are sitting there eating dinner, and you wait for her to say she has to use the restroom, because women always have to use the restroom. When she goes in, you wait a few minutes, then sneak in behind her, but you have to make sure she's in one of the stalls first, then look for her shoes and go into the one next to her. Try not to let her see your shoes. Then disguise your voice to sound like a woman and ask her to hand you some toilet paper because there's none in your

stall. When you hear her unrolling the TP, put the ring in your hand and reach under her stall. Then say in your own voice, 'I know you're in the middle of something right now, but will you marry me Kendra?' They all laughed.

♥ <u>Chapter 41</u> ♥

*T*rey called Kendra and told her to dress up because they were going to a fancy restaurant. He put on a black suit and made sure he was extra fresh so he could look nice when he asked her to be his wife. He picked her up at five o'clock and they headed to the restaurant. Kendra looked incredible. She was dressed in an ankle-length black cocktail dress with a pair of sexy shoes and nice jewelry, and had her swept up in a gorgeous twist.

Kendra had no idea Trey was about to propose to her. Before the waiter brought out their meal, Trey asked Kendra to come sit on his lap for a moment. She didn't have a problem with it because they were seated in their own little private, romantic area as he had requested when he made the reservation. Kendra walked over and sat on his lap. Trey looked into her eyes and gently brushed her face.

He was holding the ring in his other hand. "Kendra, I thank God for sending you into my life. You are a beautiful person inside and out and everything that I want in a woman. You are a loving, caring, smart, beautiful person, and most importantly, you're a woman who loves God and wants to do His will. I find that so attractive, because I know a woman like you can help keep me on track and moving in the right direction."

Trey put the ring in his other hand so Kendra could see it. "Kendra, I want you to be my wife. Will you do me the honor of marrying me?" Trey kissed her on the forehead.

Kendra was shocked. Her lips were slightly parted and she could hardly speak. She just sat there trembling as she watched him remove the ring from the box. Tears filled her eyes.

"Trey, I don't know what to say."

"How about *yes*." Trey smiled.

"You're so crazy," she said as she nudged him. She looked into his eyes. "Trey Boston, I would be honored to be your wife. Yes, Trey, I will marry you." She smiled from ear to ear. They hugged for a while, then shared a passionate kiss.

As they ate dinner, they laughed as Trey told her about Sean's idea for the perfect proposal. They talked about their future plans and whether they wanted to set a wedding date right away.

After they talked about the wedding, Kendra told Trey that her father would be coming home from jail in about a week and that she was so excited. She said she'd been looking for apartments for him and had found one in the Timonium area and rented it in her name. Her father had given her some specifics on the kind of place he wanted. Rob still had some money in the bank, even though quite a bit of it had gone to help take care of Kendra while she was still in high school living with her aunt. The rest went to pay for Kendra's college education. He still had enough left to get him by until he found a job and could get on his feet.

♥ <u>Chapter 42</u> ♥

*K*endra wanted to wait until her father came home to tell him about her engagement to Trey. She didn't have to wait very long, because that day had finally come and she was driving to the jail to pick him up.

When she pulled up he was walking out of the prison with a brown paper bag in his hand. Kendra jumped out of the car and ran to hug him. "Oh, Daddy, I'm so happy you're out of this place," she said as she hugged him.

"I am too, baby. I thank God for this day," Rob said as he hugged and squeezed his daughter.

During the drive home, Kendra told her father all about his apartment in the Timonium area. She told him it was exactly what he was looking for.

When they arrived at his new place, Kendra already had the key so they went in. Inside there was a bed that she'd picked out and had delivered and some other necessities. Rob liked the apartment and thanked his daughter. They then went to the store to get some groceries and ran a couple of errands like shopping for new clothes for him and getting a computer. It felt so good to be with her Dad again.

Kendra then took Rob to have dinner at a seafood restaurant, so he could get some crabs-something he said he missed so much. As they were eating at the restaurant, Kendra decided that her father could handle the news of the engagement and told him. Rob was very happy when he heard the news. He congratulated Kendra and told her that he wanted to congratulate Trey in person.

Tony and Sheila were planning to throw an engagement party for Trey and Kendra. They wanted to have the family go to church first and then go to Emanuel's for a celebration. They had Todd fly home for it. Trey told Kendra he wanted to personally invite her father to the party.

Rob had already spoken with Trey in person and congratulated him. They had a man-to-man talk when they went out for some crabs one night. They talked about marriage and what Rob wanted for his daughter. Rob told Trey about the mistakes he'd made in his marriage and in his life. He told him that if he could do it all over again he would take back all the wrong he'd done and be the best husband that he could be. He said he had prayed hard and asked God for forgiveness and promised the Lord that if He ever blessed him with another wife that he would be the husband that God wanted him to be.

Trey and Rob had a great conversation. Trey then invited him to church with the family and to the engagement party they were having later that evening. Rob said he would let Kendra know if he planned to attend.

On Sunday morning, Kendra called her Dad to see if he wanted to ride with her to church. Rob told her he didn't think he was going to go to church with them. He said he didn't know if he was ready to see Tony and Sheila Boston and that he would probably go to the church he'd been going to since he came home.

Kendra was disappointed but didn't push. She knew if she

was patient, God would work everything out between her dad and Tony.

Kendra drove to Trey's house so she could ride to church with him. Everyone made it to church on time, including Sean and Joe. They were all sitting together in the same pew and completely filled it. Tony sat on the end close to the aisle, then it was Sheila, Todd, his friend Brittney, Trey, Kendra, Kim, her boyfriend from the hospital named Mario, Sean and his girl, and Joe and his girl.

The service was really good and the pastor preached on the subject of forgiveness. He talked about how the Bible says we should forgive others and forgive ourselves. He also talked about the importance of forgiveness as it relates to shame and deliverance. He said that it's important to forgive yourself so that the shame of your past doesn't get in the way when you're trying to be delivered.

The message hit home for many people, especially Kendra, because she wanted her father to be free from the guilt of his past. At one point, Trey saw her crying a bit. He knew it was hard for her and put his arm around her to comfort her.

Toward the end of the service, as the pastor was making the altar call, Kendra and Trey saw Rob walking up from the back of the church. He'd actually come to the church and had been there for the entire sermon. Kendra broke down in tears. When Rob saw her tears, he started to cry. Then Sheila broke down because she knew they were finally letting out that pain that had been eating them up for years. She was so happy to see him in church and she knew how much it meant for Kendra.

Rob stopped when he got to the pew where they were all seated. Tony was sitting on the end and stood up. He and Rob just looked at each other for a moment and then embraced one another. Kendra let out a slight scream as she was overcome with joy. Trey held her.

"It's really good to see you, man, I'm so glad you came. God bless you, Rob, and welcome to the family," Tony said as he shook his hand and patted him on the back.

"Thank you, Tony. It's good to see you too, man. Thanks so much for being so good to my daughter. She's really crazy about you all. I know that you're a good man, Tony, and you have a very nice son."

Tony stepped out of the pew so Kendra could get out. Sheila stepped out next. She hugged Rob. "God bless you, Rob. It's so good to see you. I want you to know that I love your daughter very much," Sheila said.

"Thank you, Sheila. You've always been a good woman, and you are a wonderful mother figure for my daughter," Rob said.

When Kendra finally came out of the pew, she and her father hugged and cried. "Daddy, I'm so glad you're here," Kendra said as she wiped the tears from his face.

"Baby girl, I just thank you for never giving up on me."

Trey came over and hugged Rob. "I'm glad you're came. God bless you, Dad-to-be. Thanks for supporting me and your daughter."

"Thanks, Trey." Rob turned and walked up to the front of the church.

Kendra and Trey waited for Rob until he finished speaking to one of the associate pastors in the church. He didn't join the church, but he did receive counseling and special prayer.

Rob agreed to come to the celebration party at Emanuel's restaurant. He and Tony had a good conversation. They talked and got a chance to clear the air about the trial and other things. They both felt better when everything was out in the open.

The celebration was fantastic. It felt as if they were all family.

♥ Chapter 43 ♥

As the weeks passed, things seemed to get better and better. Sheila always told Trey and Todd that when things are tough, as they will sometimes be in life, to hold on to God's unchanging hand and pray that He will make things better. She told them to do everything they can and that God would do what they can't. She told them to never give up on their dreams no matter what and to always remember that God is within them and that God is greater than any kind of evil force that is in the world. She reminded them that's it's important to always hold on to their faith because faith means that you believe it before you see it and you know within your heart that as long as you keep walking upright and living a life that is pleasing to God, He will always make sure that you're okay.

Sheila also talked to Kendra a lot and gave her the same Godly advice. Kendra felt like she had a mother in her life again. And it was great because she thought Miss Sheila was a lot like her mother, as both of them were good, Godly women filled with wisdom.

Kendra and Trey decided to set a date for the wedding. They set the date for thirteen months into the future. Kendra asked

Miss Sheila to help her plan the wedding because she was her mom now. Sheila was truly moved by that.

They spent the next couple of months planning every intricate detail and had so much fun doing so.

Meanwhile Tony, Trey, and Rob were spending some time together doing guy things. Life was great.

One of Sheila's clients was a travel agent, and came into the spa telling Sheila about a fabulous vacation that she and her family could enjoy at a very good rate. Sheila had done plenty of business with her in the past and trusted her, so she asked to hear more about it. The agent told Sheila they could go on a quick four-day cruise to Mexico and some surrounding areas. The deal sounded very nice, so Sheila told the agent she'd discuss it with her family and let her know something.

Everyone thought it was a good idea, especially since they all felt like they needed a little getaway. Sheila told the ones who were interested to check their schedule and let her know if the dates worked. Sheila then called Todd at school to see if he could get away. The good news was that he'd only have to miss class for one day because the weekend fell in there and Todd didn't have any classes on Friday.

Tony asked Sheila if she thought it would be a good idea to ask Rob to go. They talked about it and asked Trey and they all agreed that it was a wonderful idea.

Just about everyone was able to go and they had a pretty sizeable group, which included Tony, Sheila, Rob, Trey, Kendra, Todd, Kim, Sean, and Joe.

The fun started as soon as they boarded the ship. The first thing they did was to head straight for the lunch buffet. Everybody was starving. Tony made fun of how much Kendra could eat. He said Trey was going to need a second job to afford their grocery bill. Everybody laughed.

After they ate, Sheila booked an hour-long massage. She said it was her turn to get the royal treatment since she was always giving it. While she did that, the guys headed for the casino. Kim and Kendra went browsing in the shops. The two of them had become a lot closer. Things were a little strained for a while after that misunderstanding about the bedroom scene with Kim and Trey, but they'd all put it behind them.

The days on the cruise were really nice. Sean, Joe, and Todd spent a lot of time talking to the single ladies. Tony and Sheila spent some much needed quality time together. Trey and Kendra did the same. The two of them stayed in the same cabin but had separate beds.

Kim spent a lot of time simply relaxing. She was a hard-working young woman and wanted to enjoy herself because she had never been on a cruise before. Rob had a blast. He was up practically all night, every night, doing everything from eating and partying to swimming and rock climbing. He was trying to make up for lost time, and spent a lot of time sitting on the deck staring out at the ocean. He thought about how much the ocean reminded him of what it felt like to be free—something he'd missed for so many years.

Tony woke up and wondered where Sheila was because she wasn't in their cabin. He later found her out on the deck sitting with Todd. Sheila loved her baby boy and missed him so much. She wanted to take the opportunity to see how Todd was making out in school, if he had any questions or concerns, and she wanted to have a little pep talk with him to help keep him on the right track.

She and Tony often talked to both their sons about the dangers in the world and making sure they stayed on the right course. Sheila talked to Todd about not letting anyone talk him into using drugs or anything like that. She said she was proud that he wasn't into that kind of thing and told him to make sure that he stayed away from people who use drugs.

She then talked with him about sex and the dangers of diseases. She reminded him that he should not have sex until he got married as God wanted him to. Todd agreed with her, and he said he told his friends the same thing because you can't look at anyone and tell if they have a disease, so it's best not to take any chances. Sheila told him that when he was ready for a relationship, he should find one young lady and make sure that she was a good person who loves God. Sheila asked how Brittney was making out at Spelman. Todd told her that she still liked it there. Todd thanked his mom for the talk and told her that he was smart and would stay away from doing anything that could mess up his life in any way.

After a while, Tony came outside and asked if he could join them. Sheila knew that Tony also wanted some alone time with Todd so they could have their man-to-man talk. They were probably going to touch on the same issues but from a man's perspective. Tony always made sure he talked to his sons. He wanted to equip them with everything they needed to not only survive in this world but to soar and to be all that God created them to be.

It was the last night of the cruise and Sean and Joe found some single ladies to hang out with and decided to go to the nightclub on board. Trey and Kendra joined them and as usual, Sean acted a fool.

The rest of the gang showed up later and before long everybody hit the floor, including Tony, Sheila and Rob. They all had a blast and thought it was a great way to bring the cruise to an end.

After they left the ship, Todd flew straight from Florida to Atlanta so he could get back to school the next day. Everyone else went back to work and Rob went back to looking for a job.

He'd been home for a couple of months and couldn't seem to find a good job. It was difficult for him to get the type of jobs he was interested in with his criminal record. He definitely couldn't get back into the education field because he couldn't pass the background check. He finally landed a job as a car salesman at a Toyota dealership. He knew he would make pretty good money because he was very good at talking people into things.

A couple of weeks went by and Rob was doing well in his new position. One day after work, he went to a nearby restaurant for dinner. He noticed an attractive woman sitting alone, drinking an island-style drink with a huge pineapple sticking off the side of the glass. She'd been checking him out as well. He walked over.

"Do they expect you to drink it or eat it?" he asked, trying to spark up a conversation.

She looked up at Rob, then looked down at her drink and laughed.

"Yeah, I know. The pineapple is so big, there's hardly any room for my lips on the glass," she said. They both laughed.

"Hi, I'm Rob," he said, extending his hand.

"I'm Robin, nice to meet you." She shook his hand. "Are you dining alone?" he asked.

"I sure am," she replied, smiling.

"Do you mind if I join you?"

"That would be nice."

Rob took a seat. The two of them had a pretty good conversation. She told Rob that she worked as a real estate agent and lived nearby. She told him she'd had a long day and didn't have any energy left to cook her own dinner. She talked about her two grown children, one who was in college and the other one who was married with children. As they talked, they found out that she was a year younger than Rob. He told her about Kendra and his job as a car salesman. He never mentioned his time in jail because he didn't think he needed to at this point.

They exchanged numbers as they were leaving and agreed to get together again.

♥ Chapter 44 ♥

As the months went by, Sheila and Kendra spent a lot of time planning the wedding. With the reception hall and wedding colors all picked out, it was now time to focus on the wedding gown.

It was a beautiful Saturday evening, and Sheila and Kendra had spent nearly the entire day shopping for the perfect gown. Kendra knew exactly what she wanted but didn't have any luck finding it, so they decided to call it a day.

As Sheila was taking Kendra home, Kendra started talking about who she wanted as her bridesmaids. She knew that one of her cousins would be her maid of honor and two of her other cousins and a friend from church would be her bridesmaids. She also wanted to ask Kim to be a bridesmaid, but didn't know how Kim would feel about it. Sheila advised her to talk it over with Trey, first before approaching Kim.

About two hours after Sheila dropped her off, Kendra heard a knock at the door. She was expecting Trey and as usual, he was right on time.

They were sitting on the couch when Kendra decided to bring up the subject about wanting Kim to be one of her bridesmaids.

"Trey, can I ask you something?" she asked, turning to him.

"Sure babe, whassup?"

"I have three bridesmaids but I want to have four, and I wanted to ask Kim if she would be one of my bridesmaids. What do you think about that?"

"Uh, well I don't know. I mean, what does being a bridesmaid mean exactly?"

"It just means that the person is a friend of the bride and supports her decision to marry the man she's chosen. The bridesmaids also help out with some of the wedding details, as well as planning the bachelorette party and the bridal shower. Kim and I have become much closer lately, but I wanted to ask you because I didn't know if she would want to do it or if you would want her to do it because of you all's past. Do you think she still has feelings for you deep down inside?"

"Look Kendra, I don't feel like getting back into all of that. I have no idea whether or not she still has feelings for me deep down inside, as you put it. I don't know what she thinks or what she feels and as far as her being one of your bridesmaids, that's something you need to talk to her about. Personally, I don't think you should ask her to be in the wedding. I mean, it might be a little strange to have her play that much of a role in everything. Why can't you just invite her and have her come as a guest and just have your family and friends actually in the wedding." Trey almost seemed a little irritated that she asked him.

"Wow, that was a handful. Why are you getting upset? Is there something else to the whole 'Trey and Kim' thing that I don't know about? Did you tell me everything that really happened in that room or what?" Kendra said, with a serious look on her face.

"Okay, here comes the drama," Trey said as he slid over to put some space between them on the sofa.

"What are you talking about, drama? I just asked you a simple question, whether or not you thought the girl might want to be in the wedding or not. If you must know, I asked out of respect for you and her. Number one, I didn't want you to feel uncomfortable having her that close to everything in case you didn't like the idea, and number two, I didn't want to put her on the spot by asking her if you thought she would be uncomfortable being in it. Did I do something wrong? If you ask me, you're the one causing drama because for whatever reason you seem to be awfully touchy over the situation."

Trey cut her off. "Look, Kendra, I had a long week, I'm working on a very tough case, I came over here to relax with you since it's the weekend and you've been complaining that we hadn't seen much of each other lately, and I just want to chill. I already told you that I don't think it would be a good idea to ask her to be in the wedding. I think she will gladly attend the wedding, but asking her to be in it might be pushing it. Now you can take that anyway you want, but you asked for an answer and I gave it to you. Now can we please watch the movie," Trey said with an obvious attitude.

"Hold on a minute, Trey. I do not understand why you have an attitude. I asked you a simple question. Now, I think it was fair of me to ask the question. I like Kim and everything and like I said, we are getting closer, but I know that she had a thing for my fiancée at one time. So out of respect, I ask my fiancée should I ask her to be in the wedding and he catches a freaking attitude. Why, I have no clue. What I do know is that usually when people get all defensive about something it's because they have something to hide."

Trey cut her off again. "So, what, are you building a case now, huh, Miss Law Student? You're not quite a lawyer yet. Now I am going to tell you one more time. I do not think that you should ask her to be in the wedding."

"Okay, I heard that part, Trey. What I am trying to find out is *why* you don't think I should ask her to be in the wedding. Is it because you think she still has feelings for you or could it be that you have some feelings for her that you haven't completely dealt with or that you haven't been able to get rid of?"

Kendra stared at him but he wouldn't look her way.

He shook his head and let out a sigh. "Kendra, you can't be serious. Baby, tell me you are not asking me if I still have feelings for that woman, for any woman. Okay, look, let me try it this way because we aren't getting anywhere like this. Kendra, I love you, I am marrying you, I want to spend
the rest of my life with you. However, I have a past, just like you have a past. In my past, I had one romantic evening with Kim but I do not have any type of feelings for Kim at this time. I look at Kim like a sister and I love her like a sister. You asked if I thought she might still have feelings for me and the answer is yes, I do. I believe that she may have some type of romantic feelings for me, but I couldn't begin to tell you how deep they are or what it means or any of that other stuff. I can tell you this. Kim is a very nice person and a very respectful young lady and she would never do anything to try to come on to me or to force her feelings onto me. I do think it is going to take a little while for her to move on but hopefully she will soon fall in love with someone. So again, please, do not ask her to be in the wedding and I think everything will be okay."

Kendra just sat there looking at Trey as if she couldn't believe the words that had just come out of his mouth. Tears started filling up in her eyes as they always did whenever she got upset.

"Trey, I don't understand why you think it is okay for you to say that another woman has feelings for you and then don't think that I should want to talk about it. Not to mention that this other woman practically lives next to the same house that you live in and sees you more than I do. Now, don't get me wrong, I like Kim, but I don't like Kim enough to let her come between me and my fiancée. What I mean by that is that I don't like the fact that she gets to spend time with a man she has feelings for or gets to hide behind the façade of being a housekeeper to the man I'm about to marry, the man she probably wishes deep down inside that she was marrying. This is the most bizarre thing I have ever heard of.

"First you want me to forget everything that I saw in your old bedroom and pretend that I didn't see how engaged you two were standing there looking into each other's eye and embracing each other. Second, you want me to just accept the fact that the woman has romantic feelings for you and gets to spend beaucoup time with you."

Kendra got up and walked into the kitchen.

Trey stood up and put on his jacket.

"Where are you going?" Kendra yelled.

"Home," he said, walking toward the door.

"Oh, how convenient you're going home, and I'm sure she's right next door, isn't she?"

Kendra ran to block the door so he couldn't leave. "Tell me, Trey, does she tuck you in at night? Huh, does she run your bathwater or give you a massage or kiss you goodnight?"

"Kendra, you have just shown me that like all women you too have drama. You have also shown me that you still have a lot of trust issues that you need to work out and I don't think it stems from me. I think it comes from your past. I hope our pre-marital counseling can work that all out." He tried to gently push her aside.

"Trey, please don't leave. I'm sorry, that was a low blow and I shouldn't have said that stuff. Come on, let's talk about this. Baby, look I am just stressed out with school and work and trying to plan the wedding, not to mention I'm on my period right now, so I'm acting a little crazy."

Kendra put her arms around him and backed him up until he fell onto the sofa.

"Trey, I'm sorry, you didn't deserve all of that. Baby, I know you're stressed out as well with working on that tough case and everything. I know that's why you're a little irritable. Look, I understand everything that you're saying about the situation with Kim. I asked you for your opinion, you gave it to me, and then I beat you up over it. You said you didn't think it would be a good idea to ask her to be in the wedding, so it's settled.

"I will not ask her to be in it. I will keep the three bridesmaids that I have and I will leave well enough alone. Most importantly, I will start practicing not giving my future husband a hard time and being a little more submissive and not so combative," Kendra smiled and kissed him on the cheek. "I love you, baby," she said as she cuddled up next to him.

"Okay, I love you too. Now can we please finish watching the movie?" Trey put his arm around her.

"Yeah, it is a good movie."

"Well, thanks to you, we were about to make our own movie, a good ol' drama flick, starring Kendra Stewart as the Drama Queen." They both laughed. "But seriously Kendra, you know we're not going to have any drama in our marriage, don't you? I'm telling you now so you can condition your mind because I'm a drama-free man and I like a drama-free woman, if such a thing exists. I'm not saying we won't have issues, but we're going to pray about things and work them out in a Godly fashion so that there's order and not a whole lot of arguing and yelling at one another. I don't believe in that because number one, it never resolves anything, and number two, it does nothing but show a lack of self-control," Trey said as he laid back to once again get comfortable on the couch.

"Trey, I agree. I don't like a lot of hollering and screaming either. I think it's silly and immature. I also like the fact that you want us to work our issues out biblically, because that's what I want as well. Besides, I think you have a lot of leadership qualities and you're a very fair person and a rational thinker. If we combine those qualities with Godly principles, then we'll be just fine."

♥ <u>Chapter 45</u> ♥

*R*ob was enjoying his job at the dealership. His sales were good and after just a few months on the job he became top salesman of the month. He was given a few extra perks for that accomplishment, including an SUV to drive as a demo. He really liked it and rode around with the sunroof open even when the weather was a little cool. He said riding around and being able to look up at the sky represented freedom just like the ocean and he liked that very much.

He'd worked all week, and it was finally Saturday afternoon. He had just an hour left on the clock and then he was going on a date with Robin. They'd already gone out a few times and he really enjoyed her company. Robin seemed like an easygoing woman and was very nurturing and understanding, both qualities he liked in a woman, both qualities that Kendra's mother possessed.

Rob left work and stopped by the cell phone store to pick up his new phone. Things had changed a lot since he'd been in jail. People weren't walking around with pagers anymore. Nowadays you had to have a cell phone, and if it didn't look like a mini-computer with touch screen and a keypad, it wasn't much. He bought himself a nice phone and immediately sent Kendra a text message. Kendra laughed when she got it and sent a message back. "Good, now I can keep up with your every move, Dad."

He laughed when he read it.

Rob was meeting Robin at the movies. She hadn't given him her address so he couldn't pick her up from her house. Rob actually admired the fact that she was taking her time and not giving up too much information or anything too fast. He believed that women had to be careful when meeting new guys they didn't know anything about.

They were both on time and met at the front of the theater. Rob felt like a teenager going on a date. He also felt like he was getting a brand new start and it felt good. He knew he was living proof of the fact that God is a God of second chances and that no matter what a person has been through, God could restore them completely.

Rob and Robin were watching a thriller and she was a little jumpy, so he put his arm around her. After the movie they went to get a bite to eat and then headed to a billiards spot to shoot some pool. He was a really good pool player before he went to prison and was glad to see that he hadn't lost his touch. They had a very nice date.

♥ <u>Chapter 46</u> ♥

November 4, 2008 finally arrived. It was Election Day. People all over the country set out to vote, and the majority of them were voting for Barack Obama, hoping to make him the first African-American president.

Sheila and Tony threw a Barack Obama party at their house that night. They, like many others, were praying for his victory. Everybody was there except Todd. He had to stay in Atlanta where he was registered to vote and where he had been volunteering with the Obama campaign.

Todd had voted before November 4, because the state of Georgia had early voting. He called his mom on the day he voted as he stood in line. He was so excited that the line was so long because so many people had turned out to vote, and not one person was complaining about the long line. Many people were happy to see it. Todd told his mom he stood in line for about five hours to vote. He said when he selected Barack Obama to be president it was well worth it and that he would stand in line all over again if he had to.

On election night, Todd went to the historic Ebenezer Baptist Church, the spiritual home of Martin Luther King, Jr., where a prayer service was being held. It was a beautiful service and was jam-packed with thousands of people. Many civil rights activists were there, along with Dr. King's sister and his children. Two big screens were set up with CNN on so everybody could watch the election results. It was a very moving time, and he spent most of the night talking to his mom on the phone while he was there.

At Tony Boston's house everybody was in place for their Barack Obama Election Night Party by eight o'clock. They too were watching CNN on the family's big screen. It was such an incredible moment in history. Every time results were posted showing Obama with a lead or showing that he'd won a particular state, they all cheered. It was truly a wonderful event. Everyone was absolutely elated. Then the moment came when the words on the screen said that President-Elect Barack Obama has been declared the winner, and everyone screamed and shouted for joy. Tears poured down the faces of Sheila, Kendra, Kim, and Sean and Joe's dates. Tony and Rob also shed a tear. It was such an incredible and moving moment. The room became silent as they watched now President-Elect Barack Obama make his acceptance speech. It was overwhelming.

They felt the presence of God in his victory. There was no question that Barack Obama was truly a Godsend, the one chosen for such a time as this. As they watched his speech on television, different cutaway shots showed the thousands of people in the crowd. There was a shot of Oprah crying in the front of the crowd. The station even showed people celebrating at Ebenezer Baptist Church where Todd was. Todd made sure he was standing behind the reporter so he could be in the shot and his family screamed when they saw him on television.

There were also shots of people celebrating in Kenya.

It was one of the best moments in history, one of the best moments the world had ever seen. Some many people were proud to be alive and witness it and so proud that the first African-American family was about to live in the White House. As they watched the scores of people from all different nationalities cheering for Barack Obama, it became evident that America really could be a better nation. It was so incredible to see the number of people shedding tears of joy. There were black people, white people, Hispanics, Asians, Indians, people from every walk of life. It was truly a new day. When Barack stepped out onto the stage with his wife Michelle and daughters, ten-year-old Malia and seven-year-old Sasha, it was a surreal moment, a God-given moment.

Once they all walked off stage, the Boston family held hands and prayed, thanking God for sending Barack Obama to lead the nation. They prayed that God would protect him and his family always. They then turned to embrace one another.

Tony hugged Sheila. "I love you, baby."

"I love you too, Tony," she replied.

Trey grabbed Kendra. "I love you, baby."

"I love you too, Trey."

Mario grabbed Kim. "Give me some sugar," he said as he kissed her on the cheek.

Sean and Joe grabbed their girls and kissed them on the lips.

Rob looked around at everyone with their significant other, then he grabbed his Bible and kissed it. "Thank you, Jesus," he said as he smiled, feeling as happy, content, and fulfilled as everyone else in the room.

♥ <u>Chapter 47</u> ♥

A couple of weeks had gone by since the election and Tony and Trey decided to take a trip to Atlanta to spend a few days with Todd.

Walking on the campus of Morehouse always brought back wonderful memories for both of them. Todd was very happy to see them and took them around to meet a lot of his friends.

The next two days were really nice. The three of them got into a little bit of everything and had a great time. It felt just like old times when Tony used to take his sons out for a day of sports. Originally, Tony and Trey thought they were going to get a little R&R in Atlanta, but Todd apparently had another agenda and ran them around like crazy.

Todd asked Trey how the wedding plans were coming along. Trey told him things were going fine as far as he was concerned because he wasn't doing anything. He said Kendra and their mom were handling all that girly stuff.

"I just told Kendra to tell me what time the wedding starts and I'll be there," Trey said. They all laughed.

Todd drove Tony and Trey to the airport Sunday afternoon. They were glad they only had about a two-hour flight because they needed some rest after their weekend with Todd. When Tony and Trey made it home, they both went straight to bed.

Trey called Kendra the next day and told her that the pastor from his church called and left a message for them. The pastor said they needed to start their six-month premarital counseling soon because they only had six months left before the wedding. They would have to do a two-hour session on the same day each week.

They agreed that Thursday evenings were probably best for both of them. Kendra didn't have class that day and that was usually Trey's light day unless he had a trial scheduled.

It was time for Trey and Kendra's first session and neither one of them knew what to expect. Trey met Kendra at the church for their appointment.

The pastor spent most of the time explaining the purpose of premarital counseling and what the sessions would consist of. They were then given a separate survey to complete, which was designed to assess the reasons why each person wanted to get married. They then discussed the survey to see if they had similar responses to certain questions. After that the pastor allowed them time to ask questions. They then concluded the session on a positive note, something the pastor said they'd always do because it was extremely important.

The months seemed to fly by, and before they knew it, the wedding was just a few weeks away. Trey told Kendra that the real estate agent had left him a message asking about the house they'd picked out in Columbia. It was exactly like the house they'd picked out months ago, when they were just dating. Fortunately another home in that same development became available and the agent called them right away.

Trey and Kendra went to settlement for their dream house three weeks before their wedding date. It was such an exciting time. They couldn't wait to get married so they could move into that big, beautiful home.

During the weeks leading up to the wedding, Kendra was amazingly calm, probably because Sheila had basically taken over as the wedding coordinator and was handling nearly all the details. The wedding ceremony was going to take place in the family's beautiful church and Kendra had asked certain members of the choir to sing her favorite song, "Order My Steps." Sheila had the details planned perfectly, and put such a touch of class on everything that it was probably going to look like the wedding of the year.

The date was set for the second Saturday in June. Todd was home to help his mother and Trey with whatever they needed. Sean and Joe were handling the plans for the bachelor party, which made Kendra a little nervous, but Trey assured her that nothing distasteful would happen.

The day before the wedding came and it was time for rehearsal. Rob was so proud to be giving his daughter away to such a good man that he cried during the rehearsal.

Rob didn't realize that Sean and Joe could see him crying. Sean leaned over to whisper in Joe's ear. "Boy, I tell you, my man better have him a whole box of Kleenex tomorrow because you know he's gonna be crying a river. He can't even get through rehearsal." He and Joe laughed.

"That's alright man, let him cry his tears of joy. He's been through a lot and he's just happy for his daughter. It's hard for a man to give his daughter away," Joe said.

"I'll bet when you get married the girl's father will probably cry as well, only he'll be crying tears of sadness because his daughter chose somebody like you to marry," Sean said, still being silly.

"Man, just shut up and pay attention so you won't mess up when you walk down the aisle tomorrow," Joe said, shaking his head.

"Alright, I'll pay attention, but do you think they'll give me two of those bridesmaids to walk with? 'Cause you know I'm a pla-ya' man, one's not enough, especially since I'm gonna have my tux on. Man, I'm gonna be so fresh," Sean said, laughing. Joe nudged him and moved over so he couldn't talk to him anymore.

The rehearsal went well and it was time for the rehearsal dinner. It was being held at a seafood restaurant near the church. After everyone ate, Trey and Kendra stood up and thanked them all for their support.

"I can't wait to marry this man. He is the best thing that's ever happened to me and I thank God for him," Kendra said, looking into Trey's eyes. Then it was Trey's turn to speak.

"I would also like to thank all of you for being here for us now as well as in the past. I thank God for giving me this beautiful woman with whom I will get to spend the rest of my life with. Thank you for being a wonderful person. I love you, baby," Trey said as he leaned over and kissed her.

Trey and Kendra then gave out gifts to everyone. They both gave individual presents to Tony, Sheila, and Rob for being wonderful parents. They then gave Todd and Kim presents for helping out and for their support. Kendra then started giv-ing out presents to her bridal party. She gave a gift to her first cousin, who was her bridesmaid. This was the cousin whom she lived with as a teenager. Her mother was Kendra's moth-er's sister. The family took Kendra in and treated her like she was one of their own.

She then gave a present to each of her bridesmaids. Two of the bridesmaids were cousins who were also from the Jackson family. The third bridesmaid was a friend from church.

It was Trey's turn to give out his gifts to the guys. He gave a gift to Sean who was the best man. He then gave gifts to his groomsmen, Joe, Todd and his co-worker, Will.

Sean was glad the rehearsal dinner had finally come to an end, because he was eager to get to the bachelor party.

As everyone left the restaurant, the guys followed Sean and Joe and the women followed Sheila and Kim. The bachelor party was being held at a lounge downtown, while the women went back to Sheila's house.

The bachelor party was kept clean and the guys just had a good time hanging out, talking and laughing.

The women also had a good time at their bachelorette party. They ate, played games, and shared a lot of laughs.

♥ <u>Chapter 48</u> ♥

*T*he wedding day finally arrived and both Kendra and Trey were overcome with joy. The church was decorated beautifully with the wedding colors of lavender and white.

The ladies were getting dressed and having their makeup done in the back, while the guys came to the church already dressed. They arrived in a stretched hummer and were clean as a whistle. All of them looked good, dressed in black tuxedos with a lavender cummerbund and bow tie. Trey was also in a black tuxedo, but he had on a platinum vest and tie, looking just as fine as ever.

Kendra was having the finishing touches done to her hair and makeup. She stepped into her wedding gown and was absolutely stunning. Sheila and Kim agreed that Kendra was one of the prettiest brides they'd ever seen. Kendra's satin gown was strapless with a low-cut, v-neck. It was trimmed in beautiful beaded metallic embroidered lace. Her jewelry was gorgeous and her hair was swept up with a few strands hanging down for a nice classy look. She was stunning, truly breathtaking.

The moment had arrived. It was time for Kendra to become

Mrs. Trey Boston, a dream come true for both of them.

Trey made his way down the aisle. Then one by one, in their beautiful satin gowns, the bridesmaids were escorted down by the groomsmen. The little ring bearer followed. He was only three years old and cute as a button. The two flower girls then made their way down the aisle. They were also three years old and just as pretty as they could be.

Everyone rose to their feet as the bride stepped inside the doorway of the sanctuary. Rob stood there waiting for Kendra and was immediately filled with an emotional joy as he held out his arm to escort her. As they made their way down the aisle, the crowd gasped at how beautiful Kendra looked. Trey was blown away as he watched his beautiful queen coming down the aisle. He could not believe his eyes.

Rob was so proud. Both he and Kendra struggled to hold back the tears. Rob escorted her up to the front of the church next to Trey and then lifted the veil off her face.

Trey and Kendra had written their own vows and became choked up when they read them to one another.

Then those wonderful words came from the pastor's mouth: "I now pronounce you man and wife. You may kiss your bride."

Trey and Kendra shared a long kiss before turning to face their guests. Everyone applauded as the newlyweds proceeded to jump over the broom. As they walked out, their guests clapped, smiling and blew bubbles.

Later at the reception, Mr. and Mrs. Trey Boston shared their first dance as they looked into each other's eyes, clearly in love. Trey whispered in his wife's ear, "I can't wait to get you home tonight. I want to make love to you so bad. I love you, Mrs. Boston."

"I love you too, husband."

The reception lasted for four hours and was incredible. The newlyweds were loaded with gifts to take to their new home.

Tony, Rob, and Todd took the newlyweds' presents to their

new house in Columbia. The couple arrived a few minutes later. Trey tried to rush his father, Rob, and Todd out of the house but Rob kept talking. Tony finally realized what Trey was trying to do and told Rob they had to go because Sheila was waiting on him.

Trey and Kendra laughed when they left out.

Trey turned to Kendra. "Now I get to have you all to myself, wifey." He picked her up and carried her up the stairs. He managed to get up five steps and had to put her down. "You must have eaten too much at the reception," he said, laughing.

"Get out of here, Trey, you're just trying to save all your energy for the bedroom," Kendra said, laughing with him.

Once inside the bedroom Trey pulled Kendra close to him and looked into her eyes. "I must tell you again, you are an incredibly beautiful bride. I was blown away when I first saw you in this gown, Kendra. I love you so much, baby."

"Thank you, Trey," she said, smiling at her husband. "And I would like to tell you again what a handsome groom you are. I love you with all my heart."

Trey kissed his new bride passionately. He tried to quickly get her out of that gown but was having a hard time. After about two minutes, she was finally able to step out of it and Trey did the rest. Once he had his new bride completely unclothed, he picked her up and carried her over to the bed. He started taking his own clothes off. He couldn't take his eyes off his wife's naked body. "I want you so bad, Kendra," he said. He tried to move as quickly as he could.

"I know, Trey, because I want you just as bad," Kendra said with a look in her eyes that was begging her husband to take her. Trey got on the bed beside her. They shared a few passionate kisses and after a few moments, he started making beautiful love to his new wife. The love-making was incredible as they released sounds of passion.

Afterward, Trey held his wife close to him as he looked into her eyes. "Baby, that was amazing. I'm so glad we waited until after we got married to make love. We really committed ourselves to it, and I'm so proud of that, Kendra. I know there were times when we wanted to make love, but we didn't slip up, not once, and it seems like our relationship was really blessed because of that.

"In some ways, it seems like it made me have more respect and appreciation for you as a woman of God and as the woman I wanted to love even more." He kissed her on her forehead.

"I feel the same way," Kendra said, looking up at her husband. "Even though I felt like I wanted to make love to you sometimes, I felt even better knowing that I was pleasing God by not fornicating. It made me feel safer with you, like you really loved and cherished me and wanted to be with me for the person that I was and not for my body. I looked at you in a different light. I saw you as my King and the man I wanted to love forever."

Trey leaned over and kissed his wife. They talked and laughed for a few minutes and then made love all over again.

It was after eleven o'clock the next morning when Trey and Kendra finally woke up. They were both exhausted from their wedding and from making love all night long. They almost felt too tired to get on the plane and head to their honeymoon, but knew they could rest once they got to Hawaii. Kendra figured they'd be tired from the wedding so she booked an evening flight so they wouldn't have to wake up so early in the morning.

"Good morning, Mr. Boston," Kendra said when she saw Trey open his eyes.

"Good morning, Mrs. Boston." He pulled her closer to him. "I can really get used to this," he said as he started touching her.

"Get used to what?"

"Get used to sleeping with a beautiful, sweet woman every night and waking up next to her in my arms every morning."

"Well, I can used to this too," Kendra said as she played with Trey's eyebrows.

"What can you get used to?"

"I can get used to my wonderful, loving husband holding me every night and keeping me safe, and then treating me like a queen every day."

"Oh, you got it, Mrs. Boston. Your wish is my command, and like I said yesterday in those vows, I will love, honor, and cherish you always. You have made me the happiest man alive." Trey pulled her close to him. The newlyweds then made love once again.

♥ Chapter 49 ♥

Trey and Kendra were exhausted by the time they finally arrived in Maui, but were immediately invigorated when they stepped outside the airport and sensed paradise in the air. Neither one of them had ever been to Hawaii before, which made it extra exciting.

They picked up their rental car and drove to the Ritz-Carlton Hotel where they were staying. It was quite a scenic route and they could see the beauty of the island with its exotic palm trees and beaches. They marveled at how captivating and exhilarating the weather was.

They pulled up to their resort hotel and were quite impressed. Everything about the Ritz-Carlton was first class. Their room had a walkout patio that led directly to the beach. It was absolute paradise.

The newlyweds spent the day unpacking and settling in. Trey opened the patio door and relaxed in front of the television, while Kendra checked out information on sightseeing tours and things to do.

The two of them decided to take a nap and wait until it was time for dinner to shower and dress. They'd already made reservations via the concierge to dine at an upscale restaurant on the island.

When it was time for dinner, Trey escorted his wife out of the room and to one of the best restaurants on the island. It had a romantic setting with gorgeous chandeliers and fire coming from the lamps on each table.

The two enjoyed an exquisite dinner and shared a champagne toast. They stayed at the restaurant for about two hours and then headed back to the hotel.

When they arrived back at the hotel, they took their shoes off and walked on the beach, still dressed in the dinner outfits. The moonlit beach was beautiful and the air was breathtaking. They walked to the edge of the sand to allow the water to cover their ankles.

"This is incredible, truly paradise," Kendra said as she smiled at her husband. I will treasure this moment." She wiggled her toes in the water.

"You know, my parents always taught me to appreciate everything and to never take anything for granted. Right now I am so appreciative of the fact that God has blessed me with a wonderful wife. I'm also appreciative of the fact that He has allowed us an opportunity to experience the beauty of this island and enjoy this moment." Trey smiled at Kendra then looked up to heaven.

They walked along the beach hand in hand, breathing in the sensuous atmosphere with all its peace and tranquility. As they made their way back, Trey picked up his wife and carried her to their hotel room. Kendra laughed as he struggled to keep his feet from sinking too far into the sand while trying desperately not to drop her.

They made it to the door and he carried her across the threshold. "Better late than never," he said as he tossed her onto the bed.

They laughed and then decided to share a bottle of wine

on the patio before heading to bed. Kendra sat on his lap as they enjoyed the wine and breathed in the essence of the island. Trey then made love to his wife on the beautiful island of Maui.

♥ <u>One Year Later</u> ♥

*T*rey and Kendra pulled up to the Boston family's house. Everyone was gathered there for Tony's surprise birthday party. They were all out back at the pool. Trey got out of the car, then went to the passenger's side and opened the door. He helped his wife out of the car and then reached into the backseat to get the twins. Kendra had given birth to the babies just two months ago. Trey often joked about how she became pregnant when they were making all that love in Maui. He attributed it to the fact that they were making up for lost time since they'd refrained from sex before marriage.

They felt blessed to have their twins, a boy and a girl.

Sheila was so excited when they arrived at the house with the twins. She and Tony just lit up every time their grandchildren came around. Before long everybody was all over the babies. Their names were Trey and Tierra and they were adorable. Todd helped Kendra carry the babies upstairs so she could put them to sleep.

It was just about time for Rob to bring Tony home and everybody was getting into place in the yard so they could surprise him. Todd had a time trying to hide all the cars down the street so Tony wouldn't suspect anything.

"Okay everybody, quiet, here they come," Sheila said when she saw Tony's truck pull up. The guests tried to hide behind the bushes and tables so Tony wouldn't see them when he walked out back. Sheila was in the kitchen when Tony and Rob walked in. Rob said he had to use the bathroom and then snuck out back with everyone else. Sheila told Tony she thought something was wrong with the pool and pretended that she wanted him to take a look at it. He followed her out to the yard.

"Surprise!" everybody yelled as he stepped onto the patio.

"Oh my goodness, what in the world is going on here?" Tony asked as he saw all the faces of his family, friends, and co-workers.

"Happy Birthday, baby," Sheila said. She threw her arms around her husband.

"Wow, this is quite a surprise. I had no idea. Now I see why Rob was acting so nervous and constantly checking his watch. I thought he had a date or something, but looks like he was in on the surprise too." Tony laughed. "Thanks, everybody, this is really nice."

The party was going very well and the guests were having a wonderful time eating, mingling, dancing and swimming. Sheila was the perfect hostess.

Kim told Sheila that she and Mario had a special announcement to make and Sheila told the DJ to give them the microphone.

Mario took the mic. "Can I have everyone's attention please," he said, waiting for the guests to quiet down before continuing, "Kim and I are getting married. I proposed to her yesterday and she accepted." Mario put his arm around Kim and they shared a kiss.

Everybody congratulated the couple and wished them well.

When it was time to cut the birthday cake, Tony said instead of making a wish, he wanted everyone to hold hands and bow their head for prayer. He took his wife's hand on one side and Todd's hand on the other side.

"Precious Father, we come to you in the name of Jesus. Lord, we give thanks to you for all the blessings you have bestowed upon us. We thank you, Lord, for our family, our health and strength, and for fellowship, oh God. Lord, we thank you for keeping us safe as we go to and from. Thank you for this opportunity for us to share love and spread joy amongst our family and friends. Lord, thank you for keeping us from all seen and unforeseen danger. We thank you, Lord, for directing our paths. Thank you for our beautiful grandchildren. They are such a blessing and a wonderful gift from you, Lord. We ask that you continue to teach us how to walk in a way that is pleasing in your sight. It's with all honor and praise that we pray to you in the name of Jesus. Amen.